Reading the stories of Guy J. Jackson is like embracing your long-lost best friend while they play Rachmaninoff 3 with one hand - at once joyous and familiar and extraordinary. Read them in your head on the morning tube and baffle commuters with the knowingness of your smile. Take a pal and a bottle of cheap whiskey to a cove and howl them to the sea. Slip them on like a pair of delicious mind-slippers at nightfall. These are tales for everywhere, for every day, for falling into and in love with again and again.
— **Gwyneth Herbert**, *The Sea Cabinet* and *All the Ghosts*

In a review of the 2012 album *Notes On Cow Life* for *Wire* magazine, legendary journalist Byron Coley described Guy's words as 'genial surrealism ... probably quite enjoyable when wrecked'. I'm quoting him verbatim as I really couldn't have put it better, and frankly, he carries far more clout than I ever could. I heard Guy's words a long time before I ever saw them written down, that amiable croak of a voice booming tales of the uncanny from stages in cramped rooms above pubs or across the London airwaves on cult radio station Resonance FM. But reading these stories now, I hear that unique voice once again. You'll hear it too.
— **Robin the Fog**, *Secret Songs of Savamala* and *The Ghosts of Bush*

A playful collection brimming with wonderful characters, sharp observations and poignant moments.
— **Sam Rawlings**, *Lazy Gramophone*

A joy to read, lyrical and evocative, subtly disturbing.
— **Danny Chidgey**, *Lazy Gramophone*

What People Are Saying About

It'll Be Fun You'll See

Samuel Beckett, Donald Barthelme, and Steve Martin, welcome Guy J. Jackson to your ranks, your new brother in the art of the absurd, the poetic, and humor. I simply loved this book!
— **Michael Elias**, author of *You Can Go Home Now* and screenwriter of *The Jerk*

The literary form, the short story, has always captivated me with its ability to create a complete world with an economy of language. In one sitting, the reader can be transported, intellectually stimulated, and emotionally moved. Guy J. Jackson's short stories do just this... he grabs the reader and delivers a visceral, psychological, and emotional experience in one quick sweep. His images are deep and satisfying and he finds a way to both open your mind and break your heart.
— **Lisa Chess**, actor, acting instructor, and director

Guy is one of the most creative and interesting writers I've worked with, almost Kurt Vonnegut in style, a pleasure to read and see where his quirky choices lead
— **Hank Braxton**, producer, director, and writer of works such as *Snake Outta Compton* and *Unnatural*

Guy J. Jackson is a consummate storytelling guy. Masterfully weaving surreal narratives that are both starkly funny yet disturbingly and deliciously disquieting. Filled with characters that inhabit landscapes of visceral absurdity often earnestly employed in the inane. Focusing the reader in on the everyday mundane horror and the apophenic scramble to form understanding that expose the injustices and dissonances that conformity brings. Yet within his tales he offers a cathartic emotional release and demonstrates a compassionate and empathic humanity.

— **Ernie Burns**, poet and author of *The Impotence of Being ... Earnest*

Praise for *Drink the Rest of That*

I've waited years for this book. Guy J. Jackson is a prolific writer of stories that combine dark comedy and tender beauty, populated by extraordinary characters rooted in the ordinary threats of the universe. Imagine if a Kurt Vonnegut-Richard Brautigan hybrid had written *The Phantom Tollbooth* and you are somewhat close to the uniqueness of this book: an old man contemplates existence through the holes in a washing machine; Elton suffers the consequences of living in a house with no clocks; a bank teller whose sideline as a stripper always results in the wrong kind of boyfriends. *Drink The Rest of That* is a dazzling, heartbreaking, laugh-aloud collection that will leave you wanting more. I'm just hoping there will be another 25 volumes.

— **Nathan Penlington**, author of *Choose Your Own Documentary* and *The Boy in the Book*

Guy J. Jackson's creaking mahogany voice resonates in every word of these absurd, dark, delightful, unexpected, abnormal, rich, indulgent, Beefheartean, nightmarish, suburban, Ionesco-esque stories, vignettes, and things. He'd be a brilliant babysitter for children who'll never sleep again. "Read me another, Mr. Jackson," they'd cry.

— **A.F. Harrold**, author of *The Point of Inconvenience, Harold*, and *Flood*

It'll Be Fun You'll See

a short story collection

Previous book: *Drink the Rest of That*
ISBN: 9781782796350

It'll Be Fun You'll See

a short story collection

Guy J. Jackson

ROUNDFIRE
BOOKS

London, UK
Washington, DC, USA

CollectiveInk

First published by Roundfire Books, 2024
Roundfire Books is an imprint of Collective Ink Ltd.,
Unit 11, Shepperton House, 89 Shepperton Road, London, N1 3DF
office@collectiveinkbooks.com
www.collectiveinkbooks.com
www.roundfire-books.com

For distributor details and how to order please visit the 'Ordering' section on our website.

Text copyright: Guy J. Jackson 2023

ISBN: 978 1 80341 295 5
978 1 80341 296 2 (ebook)
Library of Congress Control Number: 2022912454

A CIP catalogue record for this book is available from the British Library.

Design: Lapiz Digital Services

UK: Printed and bound by CPI Group (UK) Ltd, Croydon, CR0 4YY
Printed in North America by CPI GPS partners

We operate a distinctive and ethical publishing philosophy in all areas of our business, from our global network of authors to production and worldwide distribution.

Contents

Babbled Bubbles Once

Once Helenope got into this bubble machine sales racket, selling these small machines that looked like wicker sparrows. When gassed with soap, these machines blew bubbles.

Helenope of course knew that anything with a hole in it could blow a bubble but capitalism had made sure Helenope had to sell something.

Helenope was living in London at the time and so she climbed on a bus that had "one decker and then another decker up top of that one" or so they told her when she asked about seeing above the clouds, and on that bus she took the bubble machines straight to the town of Wye, W-Y-E, in Wales.

It was there where they made Palmolive Dish Soap, the whole town of Wye hopelessly, inextricably involved with the Palmolive Dish Soap Factory at its edge.

There were several dish soap stores in the town itself, boutiques of dish soap.

Everyone in Wales and England and maybe even Scotland and Ireland knew that one went to Wye if one were intent on acquiring some ultimate strain of dish soap.

So, it weren't a difficult math problem, as far as Helenope was concerned, to reckon that there were would with the bubble machines, there in Wye.

Bad news, though, the people of Wye **hated** the bubble machines.

Said they were too fancy.

Hated Helenope's sales technique of spreading bubbles all over the town square.

They hated Helenope herself, for she had a stronger Canadian accent at the time, and historically Canadians had done far less better versus the English than the Welsh had done, and people always hate seeing themselves mirrored in a minor key.

Helenope gave up and walked out of town on day three. She'd meant to make it eight days, but she had these Hippie Townswomen of Wye, also embittered with capitalism, all set up there beside her portable bubble machine stand, these Hippie Townswomen of Wye selling their absinthe-laced elderberry juice from their wheeled, flowery, absinthe-laced elderberry juice carts. And these Hippie Townswomen of Wye taking the time to turn around and yell—**YELL!!**—at Helenope about how no one needed a machine to make a bubble.

"Well, I know, but still..." was all Helenope could think to answer but who could answer against the wind of the fury of a hippie?

So there Helenope went, at dawn, on day three, wobbling on her sore feet out the east side of Wye, her suitcase dribbling bubbles behind her.

Helenope never minded the road as she didn't have a car, and she figured she'd come to a fresh road instead of one that passed through Wye. She didn't want to have any hitchhiking conversations about how she'd done there.

And you can walk all over Wales, it's the greatest.

Helenope tramped into fields,

up hills,

down dirt paths,

over fences,

jumped brooks,

skirted herds of cows, etcetera.

Her suitcase, which had holes, wouldn't stop leaking bubbles, and she knew one of the machines was still going somewhere in there, but she just felt like walking and didn't feel like stopping to open the suitcase and extinguish the rogue.

Besides, it was the one week a year the sun came out in Wales, and the bubbles leaking from the suitcase were splendid, they caught that sun just so.

2

The herds of cows Helenope skirted seemed to like the bubbles, they raised their heads and stared and let their drool drip.

Helenope passed through a field of sheep, too, and the sheep DEFINITELY liked the bubbles. They in fact actually followed Helenope, and she had only ever experienced sheep as creatures who ran from her.

Helenope thought then how unfortunate it was that these sheep didn't walk and talk and have money and could therefore buy up every last one of the bubble machines.

That monied thought gave Helenope the idea of going to the first farmhouse she came across, but when she stood on the porch explaining to the farmer's wife about how the sheep followed the bubbles, Helenope felt a bit silly-sounding, and anyway the farmer's wife closed the door on Helenope's outstretched hand.

Yes, the weathered, wordless, sad-eyed farmer's wife shut the very door on Helenope's poor, gentle, harmless, good-willed, warmly-browned, chunk-fingered hand, her poor gentle hand with that one finger with that halfway broken-through engagement ring just barely hanging in there, her gentle hand mournfully cupping the finest specimen out of the too-many-remaining bubble machines.

Bag of Clothes

Give him, please now, a bag of clothes, and I'll make sure within it I'll put all the different clothes to one side, the ones that are different than the ones he's used to wearing, sure. I'll take his worries into consideration and find a mild form of foot-twisting, one foot twisting over one, that cold white paw hung over the branch, the cold, the thin black casual tie notched twice above the waist, Gawd, no, he can't really dress himself can he (?) and you remember how he used to be able to pick the right shirt and then run and love that Frisbee and run and throw and run and throw. You ever curl up high above a sunset that way, in the highest of the highest of the too, too high windows, glimmers on the face that are so frequent you never bother wiping them off no more? Naw, you can't fault the ache of the sky. Its loveliness burns every time there aren't too many clouds and there's some sun to have to go down. But topically, sure, if you could please just give him a bag of clothes, send him on his way. His need reminds me of my creased heart, and I don't want to have to be around that kind of reminder.

-The End-

Balance It There

Balance it there in the lock for the key. Balance it there so it doesn't fall free.

Fish spine of stairs in a sweep of green grass.

The folks of Harley waiting. Lurking. Attending at their doors for something divine to occur. For something divine.

Me, I paused at a disappointing duck pond, for a disappointing tall tin, for a taste that wasn't what it promised to be.

So balance it there in the lock for the key. Balance it there so it doesn't fall free.

-The End-

Balloon Stomach Per I, Chadwater

I, Chadwater, and my stomach like a balloon which holds within, and within its productivity, all of my sins responsible for themselves.

Each organ's swell and the meetings of the organs holding meetings, pressing against one another, pressing for pressing's sake, thereby stretching the walls physiology-wise.

I, Chadwater, who wouldn't eat for a month without eating for a year, who wouldn't eat for a day without eating for a week.

My wife bumping against garbage bins.

Twas what drove I, Chadwater, to eat.

Along the sidewalks we'd go, and she with her vertigo, her highly questionable depth perception. The garbage bins put out for collection, all covered in slickness and garbage sweat. She'd bump against them as we passed. Rub up against them like a cat against a leg, except with accidentalishness, clumsiness, thoughtlessness, except NOT like a cat rubbing up against a leg but like a far-too-carefree woman rubbing up against a filthy, filthy trash receptacle.

The thought of it and the sight of it kept myself, Chadwater, up into the night, eating.

Eating mostly cheese even though I'm a vegan.

I. Chadwater. Up nights.

Chickie Noo Le Dachapoo up nights wagging and wondering at me with night-wide pupils: *why u up night, come bed, but lend me bit of cheese as well first, then come bed, go bed, come bed, go bed...*

How could she do this to us, my wife? Her one eye crossed against itself from the operation to uncross it that failed.

Still, a handicap was no excuse to strum my, Chadwater's, nerves, and anyway I told her time and again to simply reverse the way she saw the street against the mirror of her mind. We'd be walking the sidewalks and she'd be rubbing along a wall and leaving a great black mark of soot along her shoulder-padded gown arm. Then would come a garbage bin she would bump a hip against, if I wasn't carefully looking, if I was too busy watching my stomach slosh slide-to-slide across the chafe of my belt.

How could she do it, how could she see the presences of the Dirt Haunts (?!?!) who collected cans and bottles from the garbage bins, reveling in the grime, no gloves between the dozen of them that worked this street of theirs. Cuz the street was theirs, really it was, it belonged to them, twas theirs, theirs twas.

How could she see all that and all them and still do what she did?!

Then when the garbage trucks came with their whirling-clamping mechanisms which violently dumped garbage bins into their truck bellies leaving in the air from such violence a spray of mist. Garbage Mist. You didn't want to be near that or you'd be misted with filth.

How could my wife see all that and even still see the sweat off the garbage bins as they sweated garbage in the heat of summer?

How could she, my otherwise-dear wife, see all that and still totter and bump against the garbage bins, when all she had to do was reverse those hin⬚ ⬚⬚⬚⬚⬚ ⬚⬚⬚ ⬚⬚⬚⬚⬚ ⬚⬚ ⬚⬚⬚ ⬚⬚⬚⬚⬚⬚⬚⬚⬚⬚ eye and cross to the other side of the sidewalk?

I, Chadwater, up nights eating cheese and sometimes a can of hot dogs from the otherwise-green grocery store where hot dogs come in cans, even though I was a vegan (still am) and I knew it was wrong.

I, Chadwater, up nights cleaning the bedsheets round and round in the washing machine.

Cleaning towels in the sink.

Cleaning clothes in the shower while I shower in the shower while Chickie Noo Le Dachapoo stands dutiful guard but stares with night-big pupils as in: *Why u up night in danger shower? Come bed?*

And my, Chadwater's, wife slumbering innocent in blacked windowed depths of the bedroom, sleeping so peacefully and *sans souci*-even though she's got bruises from garbage bins on not just one hip, but both.

-The End-

Banks and So On

Banks have use of helicopters and so on. Gunships, missiles, etcetera.

America is the one place where if I control my eye movement long enough, I can buy a gun.

That's why ocotillos have character. To keep from getting shot at by those who come blow, who aren't Dinah.

I should make sand of the opportunity that I don't live in Europe.

I'm not going to let you do that, find a constructive use of time.

Them eating them with their old teeth, them who are so old they can't see the way to sustainable farms because their eyes are so old, eyes so much older still than their old teeth, so much older even stiller than their eyeteeth.

What's the situation with all these beer cans on the floor of your car? as Master Builder James would ask you. Cuz he knows flooring.

Let's just drive around the block once so we can listen to this song, as DJ Ricky would say to you to avoid the question of the cans.

I feel like this could go down better with less hurt feelings.

You do realize feelings have been hurt, especially the feelings of the banks when they pretend to have them, but this is what's best for tomorrow.

And every day thereafter.

Okay, cut to the chase.

They tried to tell me how angelic children were but then I hear the children on the shuffleboard court explaining to one another who cheated, who's a baby, who played a good game as opposed to who did not, who's a bad sport, and I think how I was never an angelic child, shooting squirrels with a .22 and waving

9

my dad off moose hunting with a red and white handkerchief and prank calling a hundred dollars' worth of pizza to poor old freckled, asthmatic Michael… what was his last name? Sorry, Michael. And more sorry about the pizza, so much more sorry, still and all, about that pizza.

Or I see three children with a bouncing basketball and I know two of the children are cruelly keeping the basketball from the third. That's just automatic with children, eh? That's just par for the course with kiddos, eh? That's just de rigeur as I think the French say but then again, I get French wrong all the time, tho I get it less wrong than when I get English wrong all the time. But you see three children and you know that's always two children against one child, always. Two against one. Three against one. Four against one. Ten against one. Children. The little beasts.

Wait a minute, hang on.

I've got to stop that whale. I repent it. Tho I didn't mean whale exactly, I meant the other W word.

Okay, cut to the chase.

In the spring of August 2011, waiting hard for November 11 cuz of the numerology of 11/11/11 (SPOILER: nothing happened), I found myself listening to a lot of _____ again because I forget their name, tho they were a rock band from the earliest glimmers of my childhood realizations that I, too, could rock, and because I remembered Billy _____ who drove by in his convertible and provided badly rolled j-dawgs much to us kids' confusion and vanished spare time and also Billy _____ played about the sugar pouring at top volume or the eeee-bin-gleeee-bin-gloppin-globe-enn, because I remembered Shawn _____ walking away with his high tops untied owning the coolest ghetto blaster on Glacier Avenue and playing about the bells of the too-too-far-underground at top volume. Or wherever the bells were hanging around clanging that was a forbidden place for them to be, back then when plenty was forbidden to us kids. Top volume, yeah, in fact SO LOUD.

Yes, I was born ugly.

Raised ugly.

I've gone along until the moment of this pen on this paper ugly. (Tho you yourself are receiving this in handsome type with a slick, selected font.)

I'm going to pass on to the next life ugly.

But, hey, according to Terry Gilliam, an extremely important authority on the matter: "The world needs grotesques, too."

So, there you go, kiddo.

Point and match and set and victory, ahhhh victory.

Banks might appear to have victory sometimes.

But the victory of banks will only ever be cold and numerical, while our victory will be hot with hothouse use of hot handed emotion sparked into breathless clumps of sometimes rightly, sometimes wrongly used letters.

-The End-

Bar Boys

"You gonna water that down even more?"

"It's light beer, and I want to drink it fast."

"Ten minutes fast?"

"Ten minutes."

"I got friends who do that."

"I haven't got any friends."

"How much money you got?"

"Not much."

"With money you don't need friends."

"I don't got much money, neither."

"Well, how about I pay you to hang around with me?"

"Sure, where do we go first?"

"A bite to eat at the SIR. That's a tacky acronym for Standard Indian Restaurant."

"Okay. Let me start my half-hour goodbye."

"What do you need for that?"

"I'll need a pickle, an egg, but not the two together. I'll need a heavy beer, not a light one."

"Time enough for a heavy beer? Oooeeeooo!"

"Yeah, that's because, because of you, I now own half of an hour."

-The End-

Barley Avenue

Oh, Barley Avenue, I know that street.

Where you can go to the crumpled house hidden behind three elms.

Capture a deal of warmth with a few kind words.

With a fine daisy bouquet.

Yes, yes, yes, yes.

Old Mrs. Sutter there.

She talks of special dinners she once was at, years past.

She can remember each special dinner.

The exact dishes she ate.

How they made her feel.

Be that fulsome, or sick, or steady, or wanting.

That talent of hers for remembering what she ate at the governor's.

For remembering what she ate at the bar mitzvah.

For remembering what she ate in the hospital.

The night her daughter was born and then died.

Or maybe was never born at all.

Cuz you've never met Old Mrs. Sutter's daughter.

So you can't say.

Th̶ ̶

It shows a deceptively simple care for life.

It'd be like kicking a lamb, to poo-poo such a talent.

So, you ask if I know that street?

Sure I do.

-The End-

Barthon Park, a Poor Idea

The Barthon Town Citizenry, they got together all the torn machinery that had been rusting in everyone's farmyards over the last couple of decades and put the machinery in a field beside the road just outside of town and made a gravel-covered parking area and called the result Barthon Historical Park.

On opening day, the entire town of Barthon came to the park and everyone fired barbecues.

But the children of the town immediately began running and screaming and climbing on the farm machinery and then en masse cutting themselves and hurting themselves. Horrified, everyone with children left the opening day event.

Only grown-ups remained and they were cynics about how what was purportedly historical was really just a collection of rusting, rotting farm machinery from only 40 years earlier when technology was lame.

So, someone brought out alcohol and the adults all got bitterly, desolately drunk.

Then more people ran around and engaged in antics, more people were cut on the farm machinery and hurt, some people even had the Sexytime Time with other peoples' spouses in the cockpits (no pun intended but hey when in Rome) of some of the farm machinery and were thus all cut up in nether regions, and then there was, of course, a run on tetanus shots at the local hospital, or really an urgent care.

And because it was America in the year 2007 and no one in Barthon could afford health insurance, each tetanus shot cost its recipient a cool Four Thousand Dollars, as in $4000 (four thousand) dollars. Which, for most citizens of Barthon, was the equivalent of two months' pay.

And after all that, generally, no citizens of Barthon were ever again found in Barthon's Historical Park, and the park evolved from a dropped note of civic pride into a way of accidentally diabolically trapping tourists. Accidentally diabolically trapping tourists in a rust-crusted labyrinth of olden days farm machinery while chasing them (the tourists) with chainsaws.

-The End-

BBT

Half the pond water was sheeted with ice, and a few daredevil ducks were padding on this cover. The scene, reaching her eyes refracted through crystalline cold, gave S a capital scheme of comedy, and she rose from the bench, shook powder off her sneakers, and ran from the park and across Galena Way to the ABC.

This place, cozy with baking, had just then cracked its doors for breakfast.

S bought the least expensive loaf of bread, prizing crumples of ones from her twisted pocket, and she returned to the side of the pond within eight minutes of her departure. She checked that against her watch. It had been eight minutes there and back and buying the bread. Eight minutes was perfect.

The morass of ducks, with communal thought, sensed the loaf before she'd even wrangled it unwrapped. They started in on her, marvelous, but at one passing second a little frightening, but then marvelous again. The initial few shreds of bread fluffed onto the ice and the ducks were sure in getting after them. This was S's idea, to see their attempts on the ice. This was the great comedy. Ha, thought S, and her breath caught sound from laughter that started in her head, and that giggle of hers that she liked so much for it still being as unstoppable as a child's at times, it clattered into the park and up amongst the treetops. The ducks on the ice were there before her. The scene lay before her. Worshipful of her. Slipped-up orange triangle feet. Wings as splintered arms. Bills butting to get at the brown and white morsels. Her alone, S, had disintegrated their village to a bedlam. The ice had no thickness, and in this S hoped for further comedy of webbed feet poking holes and plunging the bundles of feathers they held down into little traps. But no luck there, since the combined weight of the ducks only brought countries of ice shearing free and sinking somewhat under the cold water, the same as dreams losing themselves in the morning. A sliver of disappointment slid in. The ducks didn't fall in holes. S's smile faltered, but then she stuck up her chin and grabbed it back. Big grin, because really a sliver wasn't much disappointment. Alright, alright, she thought. She fed the rest of the bread away. She was really watching, really timing, so timeliness put arms around her as she observed the ducks to do what they would always do. Quiet, dark water, splashings lightly disquieting the air, nipped air, with a tuck of chill, wrapped and heavy. And the sun, putting supposed first light upon brick and building that had already seen it first and first again. Her laughter had long since dropped away in the park, and her hand dropped with it, bread, bread, bread, mechanical, the sole function of the hand then, there. Put the crumbs onto the pond top. Then the ducks ate the crumbs, and their moment's purpose was only just the one thing, too.

S breathed in. Huffed breath out.

She looked to her watch, and saw she had kept time, but she had little time left beforehand. So, she found her hiding place and plucked out her bag, an affair that hung too heavy l[illegible] step lively out of the park, then from the paths to sidewalk after sidewalk to the newly-opened post office.

Inside the blinds were raised but the sun was not creeping through, as it hadn't crept first around the outside corner. There was the weeping mustache of the man behind his counter, and S bought a postcard. She stood at a counter of her own, almost too high a counter for little her, and she rested her elbows and took a chained pen and wrote her address and wrote her postcard, writing:

Dear Larry

then writing:

I'm with someone.

Then signing:

Yours,
S.

She bought a stamp to stamp her revenge.

She dropped the card in a brass mouth.

She walked further, to the OSF, went in through a glass door and up a big fat staircase and to a desk and then spoke to a girl. The girl looked into her appointment book that had once been dropped on the desk with a leather splat. Opened like a bird and then dropped satisfyingly (to the girl) when she dropped it. Or maybe not opened at all, just a book dropped but still satisfying, the click of its rings and the slap of its cover, bap, like that, or even just slid on there even, chak, chak, chak. How good would that be? As enough as the balanced account, that's how.

But, thinking of thinking that way, S had to stop thinking.

"Your name?" said the girl, or the girl was saying.

S gave her name.

"I'm sorry, I don't see your name."

S leaned in. "I had an appointment."

"Did you send us a picture?" asked the girl, or had asked. There was that time thing again. S nodded gravely.

"Let me check a file," the girl says. Then, after that said, the girl checked a file.

"I had an appointment."

The girl negotiated or negotiates or was about to negotiate. "Maybe he'll watch you anyway."

And so, while S was still digging in her bag, a man emerged and met her with a bump. She gave her name again. She had come up from her bag with an empty hand as far as getting out another picture.

"Let's go have a look," said the man next, and they went. They came into a hall, and the skylight shafted in sunlight, and the noise of a footstep returned twofold from the wood floor, from the wood walls. The man perched behind a jittery table, and S was on his level, crossing to the room's exact center and then turning to deliver. She explained a few things, how she'd thought to write what she would say, who she was supposed to be, and the reaction she hoped for. Then she began. Her belly abruptly swollen with fool fire, she spoke of tidal pools and the brief paragraphs on love within them, and then these brief paragraphs sent spellcasting into the air between herself and the passive man watching behind his brush fort of brows and brown hairs.

S sang a little, singing: *Sweet endless merciful jumping fireflies in the summer night unlike anybody who loved the machine.*

And then when S came back to speaking in rows again, it was the digression about the dark red rundown house on the hill, the casting of her sister's bones before a tree at one o'clock in the afternoon of the last day of summer, the shelves of the shed where the sad-faced baby boy slept in a cigar box, the tickle of her brother's beard on the flushed nape of her neck, the ringing of her dead father's bell while her dead father walked on the hill above the house and his dead presence blotted against every single violent sunset.

S spoke. At the beginning it was stepping out into winter, in the middle it was drowning, and then, finishing, a twist of fear came to S, who was out there at the end of the tether of her lines of talk, in a chamber at the brink of everything, and much too soon pulled back.

The man said: "Thank you very much."

S said: "Thank you."

"We'll give you a call," said the man.

And his smile said to S it had all been exciting.

S left through the same glass door so her shoes could clock on the bricks. She noted a new rip in her bag, making its way. A new threat. She hoped she had given them the right phone number. It had all been exciting. Time had been sudden. She might've given them the wrong phone number. But never mind. They'd find her, when they called, when they were all of them full up with need. They'd find her like treasures got found. They'd find her so she could finally change her dumb-dumb one-letter name to Marjorie Tripleton Lexington Aurora Butterworth Cuddlesfield.

-The End-

Be It Ye Title Bout

This is about Teddy. This is about his plan, and nothing else. Because, really, if you really think about it, it's all in the plan.

Teddy Laurents had gotten to the point where he could use his growing psychic powers to move a lightweight object. Nothing bigger than a pencil, so far. A pencil weighs what? An ounce?

With his psychic powers, Teddy wanted to be able to move three pounds exactly. That's what his wife's coffeepot filled with coffee weighed.

He'd brewed the coffee pot all full up with coffee and put it on the bathroom scale. Three pounds. Of course, he did as much when his wife was at work at the Co-Op. Of course, he couldn't let her see or ask what the hell he was doing.

So, yeah, Teddy'd weighed the coffee pot, brimming with hot coffee. He'd stood there in the quiet bathroom with groggy morning light sifting the air, looking at the marks and numbers in the scale window, wondering at himself.

The ever-so-slight leak that the tub faucet had had since time gone gave out a quick drip drop.

The coffee pot filled with water was three pounds, exactly, said the scale

So Teddy just needed to be able to move, with the power of his mind, three pounds.

Yup, yup, yup.

The things Teddy'd gotten up to since losing his job.

He practiced his growing psychic powers industriously, graduating from psychically moving a pencil to psychically moving a hairbrush to psychically moving a glass of milk. About the pursuit of greater and greater psychic powers, Teddy was so motivated! In fact, he reckoned he was a star member of the unemployed.

He didn't drink, he didn't smoke, he wasn't on any drugs. He kept the house neat-as-you-please. He was healthy. He had an ideal body weight because he didn't eat any more than a fist-sized portion of vegetables and rice at any one sitting. He wasn't a drain on the household budget. He had three outfits for puttering around as an indolent member of the unemployed, all three of which were equally composed by a pair of thick socks, a pair of plaid pajamas, and a blue bathrobe, and he daily changed these outfits and every other day washed the ones he wasn't wearing. He showered each morning. Teddy would never be caught lounging with anything beyond a fresh scent twisting in his aura.

So, yeah, once Teddy latched onto the whole developing-the-hidden-power-of-the-mind-to-thus-move-objects-with-the-mind idea, he had as much work ethic as any Olympic athlete.

And the psychic practicing, and the weighing of the coffeepot, all of it was because of his wife's cat. A calico. The calico cat was his wife's own kind, and it had free rein and every indulgence.

But as far as Teddy was concerned, the calico was hatched in some local hell.

Teddy was so enamored of his unemployment he wanted to pursue its peace and its quiet unto death, but the calico was a stain on his days.

Teddy thinks like this, he thinks: the calico cat. The calico has to be let out. The calico has to be let in. The calico has to be fed, three times a day. And the calico draws attention to its feeding time by mewling. And the calico has a litter box, which needs changing once-a-week.

Teddy thinks: This motherfucking calico cat. It just sits in the sun and has no purpose and drags on me.

Teddy wanted to be alone in his new world of unemployment.

The calico wasn't such a thorn when Teddy had been working. But now Teddy wanted a nothing, he wanted no other living presence in the house from 8 a.m. to 6 p.m., he wanted a vacuum in all the periods when his wife was at the Co-Op.

Yeah, yeah, yeah, no calico, so Teddy, alone, could wrap himself in this newly gained sense of time. This liquid time, these days without schedule. How Teddy loved their feel, these days, wherein he could coil in the armchair under the window as the warmest light came through. There, beyond the window, was the universe without, and there, back behind his eyes, was the universe within, and Teddy could bobble every sphere of each with the tentacles of his mentality. In this meditation, he could come closer and closer to the permanent capture of the feeling that would make life okay.

That one feeling, that passing insight, the one that came to him where he noticed, for only a moment, Some Big Something.

It was Something out-of-reach of his vision when he peered as hard as possible past the treetops. It was Something far below his gut, when he let his mind go inside out. It was Something. Teddy was an agnostic but he thought the Big Something was maybe even the presence of either God, or the Goddess, or both.

And if Teddy could only hold onto that Something forever, instead of it being just a fleeting glimpse, well, then, hey...

But Teddy couldn't ever grasp and hold onto the Big Something because the calico was around, and it was an albatross hung on Teddy's lifeforce.

And he couldn't just get rid of the calico without his wife divorcing him, because the calico was his wife's baby. And Teddy's wife, in turn, was Teddy's baby.

So, he had to make the end of the calico look like an accident.

And once Teddy decided that, he noticed that each morning his wife was in the kitchen making her morning pot of coffee and could be witness to the end of the calico without any suspicion that Teddy had done something wrong.

And Teddy noticed that each morning the calico took the exact same path through the kitchen and to its food dish at the exact same time, mewling shrill for a spinal anti-thrill, mewling to be fed.

Every day, the same path, from kitchen door to food dish.

And that path led the cat directly under the spot on the counter where the coffee maker sat, the calico cat passing beneath the coffee maker at always exactly the same moment the coffee maker's light switched from green to red, indicating the coffee was hot and done.

So all Teddy had to do was sit at the kitchen table, pretend to read the paper, and use his psychic powers to pull the coffee pot from the coffee maker just as the coffee was hot enough, just as the calico passed beneath, and the calico would be struck soundly on its thin skull by three solid pounds and maybe, for good measure, the pot would break open and stick the calico full of glass and boil the calico with hot coffee.

And that, Teddy figured, would be the end of the goddamn calico cat.

And that was Teddy Laurents. And that's how he was engaging himself. And that was his plan. And, as we said, it's all in the plan.

-The End-

Be the Exit, Please

I wake up in Red Bluff. My shirt and hair are soaked. In one window the ghost of the clock reads EI:E. I look through the windshield and see a long-haired hitchhiker come out of the convenience store, staring hard into a pair of lottery tickets. The tickets'll win if he stares hard enough, I think. I strip off my shirt, which is blossoming with sweat and fresh blood. I shouldn't just be sleeping out in parking lots in strange towns, I think. I panic a little. I could've gotten stabbed by some crazy fucker while I was sleeping. I need to get back on the road and fight sleep with coffee. I toss the bloody shirt on the floor in front of the passenger seat and then pluck a fresh shirt from my duffle bag in the pitch dark of the back seat. The new shirt reads AVIATOR OF TONSILS across the chest, in multi-colored letters. I take a glimpse of myself in the rearview mirror, then spy a woman bicycling by in the road behind my car. She sports a black halter top that gives me half a hard-on. I worry for her bicycling-astriding sexiness, out at this hour. I say a prayer for her. I close my eyes. I open them. The ghost of the clock reads EO:E. I think I need coffee. I start the car and the radio is in the middle of a mariachi's song. The mariachi sings **sello mento** noche essa vanseudo. I drive in the opposite direction of the freeway exit and arrive at a donut shop. There are no other buildings besides the donut shop and the convenience store. As I park in the donut shop parking lot, the woman goes by again, still on her bike. The wind from an open back window brushes me. I look back over my shoulder and I'm panicked to see the open back window. I think *What if some crazy fucker dropped in a rat that's hiding under the seat and bites me on my Achilles tendon when it gets half-a-chance. I can't be sleeping and letting my guard down in any old parking lot off any old exit along the freeway.* I struggle into the donut shop. The lights inside are on too bright. I look back at my car through the glass door and see the sign on the glass door reads pen 2 hos. Beneath the slopes of the glass cases the donuts are dried to look like monkey paws. The Dirty Filthy French Man in the back room calls out that he'll be right there. I stand in the puddle of myself. On the television in one upper corner dancing ladies that are every one of them sultry, or so it seems to me anyway, dance. My semi hard-on swells and disappears, swells and disappears. I look back at my car through the glass door. I shouldn't have left my wallet on the dashboard. I shudder to think I could have been stabbed while I was sleeping. I think *I always used to get the great sex in my charming way back in, back in, back before, back when, back* I shake my head. Then, to keep away the creeping, dawning realization I keep the thoughts to thoughts of how *I could always make them break vows of celibacy and I could always seduce them out of at least the top half of their clothes even if they had another paramour somewhere else in town* whereupon the Dirty Filthy French Man came out and from the open door of the kitchen a song warbled that was the same song, I knew, from the radio in my car and it went **elasta lila commigos y vasta tompasta y totta birna**. "What do you want?" asks the Dirty Filthy French Man who, I guess, is also le caissier and also le plongeur. I pick out three donuts like a child, deciding like a child in a hard stare through the glass at the sugar, like donuts and the child, like the comfort of childhood at the heights of a single sugar crystal pricking pinpointed through glass. I pick out a size of coffee, deciding like a grown-up. Through the glass door comes a white man, whitened to translucence, and with dark hair in shifting coils, with a big, bare fish belly, with no shirt beneath a leather sleeveless jacket, with pants of thin cloth for lounging in the Mediterranean, or in the heat of Red Bluff, and the white man's also coated with a film that blurs him and marks him as bad and crazy and a fucker. And the white man has a knife, bouncing against a thigh, with a blue mesh holster. I produce a twenty-dollar bill, and the white man is now close behind me, even closer, that I have to reach around the white man's presence to get a lid for the coffee, to get a straw to stir the sugar. The white man is against my back when I get the overdose of change that comes from a twenty-dollar bill clashed against the cheap three donuts and the cheap coffee. I pray that the white man doesn't get any bright ideas from the sights and the lights and the glinting of all that change. I wake up. Ghost clock. Bloody shirt. Lucky hitchhiker. Halter top and half-a-hard-on. Dry donuts. White man. Meshed knife. Bright change. I am driving, tasting at coffee like soap, eating a donut like the dried-up old lopped-off paw of a fucking monkey. My car passes the woman in the halter top on the bicycle. She is heading in the opposite direction. I say a prayer for her in all foreign words. I reach the entrance to the freeway. A cluster of hitchhikers stand around the sole metal leg of a light pole, each of their two dozen faces in cowls of shadows. I say no way to every jerked-up thumb. My car joins the stream of the freeway. The mariachi on the radio sings the entire worldwide history of STFU singing **seula la mento commigo massada esta ladda donde;** a rat under the seat bites into my ankle. I squeal but grit my teeth and hold on till the next exit. I exit. I scream and scream and scream and surprise myself because I do so much ᛁᚱᛁᛗᛄᛁᛁᛁᛁᛁᚿᛁ, ᛁᛁᛁᛁ ᛁᛁᛁ ᛁ ᛁᛁᛁᛁᛁᛁᛁᚿᛁᛁ ᛁᛁᛁ ᛁᛁᛁᛁᛁᛁᛁᛁᛁᛁ ᛁᛁᛁᛁᛁ ᛁ ᛁᛁᛁ ᛁᛁᛁᛁ ᛁᛁᛁᛁᚿᛁᛁᛁᛁᛁᛁ ᛁᛁᛁ screaming because my center is soft and if I believe in evolution then I'm forgiven for screaming because I'm just like any other animal. The car cloverleafs, heading back for Red Bluff. I tug at my shirt to think about wiping my ankle but the shirt is already too bloody. I wake up in Red Bluff in the convenience store parking lot. In the window the ghost of the clock reads ES:E. I think *I could've been stabbed by some crazy fucker* as I think how *those are most of my fingers amputated and strewn on the dashboard like seven fancy hot dogs.* I start the car. A hitchhiker comes out of the store with a fistful of lottery tickets. He'll win if he squeezes hard enough. There is a mariachi on the radio. While the mariachi sings **mooola maleeleelee malinglinglunglung malunglunglunglunglunglunglunglunglunglunglunglun glunglunglunglunglunglunglunglunglunglunglunglun glunglunglunglunglunglunglunglunglung**, I think about getting a donut and coffee. My shirt is damp with blood. I take it off, and rub some blood in my hair, and jerk at my hair with both hands, and my three remaining fingers, using the blood to make my hair sticky and freshly tousled-looking, and most especially cool-looking in case I ever stop the car and talk to that woman in the halter top on the bicycle.

-The End-

Beard and Mustache Championships

ITEM: It was The First Ever Beard and Mustache National Championships this week and this reporter should've, of course, capitalized on that by going and reporting journalistically about the championship, capturing each nuance and each revelation of character, but except for, of course, this reporter's disgust with body hair, garnered from a young age and continuing hitherto. Nowadays, this reporter avoids hair in all forms and lives in a state of forced/self-induced alopecia, which is actually called trichotillomania, technically speaking, for being self-taught. This reporter used to stand in the showers as a young boy in the local locker room of the local pool and look at the hairiness besieging grown men around this reporter and think about how this reporter would *never* go there. *Body hair*, thought this reporter back then, *thanks, but no thanks.* The thought of a mouthful of hair, or a bucket of hair. Someone had once told this reporter about "a bucket of hair" and that was the last this reporter ever needed to hear of that concept. Hair. The unruly sprouting. So, it's unfortunate to some, this reporter is sure, for this reporter to say as much, but this reporter will not be covering the story of the men who grow hair for a hobby and then enter a championship to champion whether their hair has grown more better than the other men's hair, the other men who grow hair for a hobby. But this reporter did see them from afar, the champions and the would-be champions alike, when they made themselves a parade through the town, a sort of hair parade. This reporter took one quick nauseous look from down this reporter's dirt road when their parade passed by this reporter's ranch where this reporter lives apart. They seemed friendly, and they bore flags, but they did buckle this reporter with nausea. This reporter fell to his knees and begged God not to make him eat all that hair. Because what if that somehow happened? DATELINE: 4/60

-The End-

Beneath

Finding her shoulders beneath her orange shirt was finding sheer heaven.

Put yourself in Beasley's eyes of Beasley's mind, please and please.

On the after-party occasion the cop came along Beasley's way while Beasley found her shoulders beneath her orange shirt again and again, way deep back in his transmitter, way deep back in a December, way deep back when.

"I can't drink wine on my own front steps?!" Beasley was incredulous and then he's way back deep down deep to finding her shoulders beneath her orange shirt.

"Nope, not in the city," said the cop, writing in his ticket book while Beasley lost interest in cops and their doings and found those shoulders (not the cop's shoulders cuz the cop was a big filthy Fascist Caucasian male motherfucker) beneath her orange shirt and Beasley watched the cop write and found her shoulders beneath her orange shirt back when he'd found her shoulders beneath her orange shirt and then asked her if he could put his arm around her shoulders and then she said yes and then he (Beasley, not the cop) put an arm around her soft, soft shoulders, finding them somewhere beneath her orange shirt back, back, back, back, back, back, back, back, back, back when.

Beasley then sat finding her shoulders beneath her orange shirt with the ticket in his hand, after the cop hand was gone.

And after the cop in and of himself was gone and Beasley's double-decker wine bottle in the shape of a bus from London to High Barnet had been poured out into a gutter by the hand of the gone Fascist cop and handed brusquely back to Beasley's other hand, Beasley's hand without the ticket in it, and now with the empty wine bottle in it and so now then the wine river lay in the gutter like a long lost river in some exotic somewhere threaded with rouge rivers, somewhen in the long ago deep deep deep deep past, somewhere where Beasley might still find her soft, soft, still soft shoulders just there shouldering up his sloppy arm from beneath her orange shirt.

-The End-

Benton, Sir, Excuse Me, Mr. Benton: A Sequel Pitch for Your Fine Film

Nadine went to the chop shop and had Bedford drill an actual hole in her head and insert a bolt. This was, of course, after Nadine had read too much Mary Shelley.

"I don't know, Nadine, this might hurt," said Bedford, readying the drill.

"I, above all, don't feel pain per se," said Nadine.

"Well, I'm up for it if you are," said Bedford, and drilled the hole.

After the bolt was inserted and the wound around it had healed, Nadine began wandering in thunderstorms, waiting and hoping for lightning. She found high grassy plains to walk on, thinking how great it might be, lightning filling her skull.

Maybe the lightning wouldn't even kill her.

Maybe it would scorch her brain in such a way as to make her some kind of superhero with superpowers. Then she could be impervious to pain, perhaps. Or turn war into peace. Or at least always agree the color of her skin with the color of her dress.

In the kitchen Nadine had her back to Gilles, and was clutching the wine bottle thinking *here I go, I can't help it but I guess I'm going to just go ahead and restart the argument about the corkscrew even though it was done with twenty minutes ago.*

Tending bar, Nadine wends her way through the faces leering up from chairs bobbing in a sea of smoke.

Veronica of the green grass coat, thought Nadine.

Marvin's marvelous tea bottle indeed, thought Nadine. He'd told her it never needed refilling and was originally filled with fake orange juice.

Gilles' clumsy hand on the undercarriage of her thigh.

In that moment Nadine knew that Marvin felt he could trust her when he pointed out that DJs were a lonely lot, lonely for girls to request songs of them, and that she should thus be the ambassador in going to request an ABBA song.

Dickens characters in little pictures on the wall, Nadine noted, as she made her way through the pub.

Even though Bedford was plenty alive, with the energy and verve to run from police and hop fences, he had a ghost face, and made the perfect drug dealer. He never minded Nadine's craziness, neither, and would lay a tattoo anywhere she asked, stick a piercing anywhere she asked, impale a bolt into her skull.

Nadine drank a bottle of wine all to herself, and felt little.

In the Southern Tunnel, Nadine passed the same dreary homeless man day upon day upon day upon day until one day her heart cracked because she no longer saw the homeless man's dog stretched on its blanket by the homeless man's side, no, she only saw the blanket.

Nadine was riding on the train when Marvin spoke up and said: "I'm gonna screw you silly when we get home." He sounded very sweet about it, but she thought about how the remark would look crass on paper. Nadine blushed for a moment because everyone had heard, but then she thought well, what's their problem, doesn't everyone have sex at one time or another, so what's so amazing about it anyhow?

Then a woman said: "I wish someone was gonna screw me silly when I get home."

And a man near the woman said: "I'll do it."

And the woman said: "Okay."

And the pair of them blushed as well, for a single very long minute, before finally getting off at the Hillbottom stop together, everyone around them on the train knowing what they were gonna go do, and Nadine and Marvin pleased in the knowledge their loose-lipped love had maybe, maybe, maybe, maybe caused more love for absolute strangers.

The train incident with the strangers was an amazing coincidence, besides, because it happened to be the very same way Nadine's parents met.

Nadine once lived with Danny Bilbau, whose parents had gotten married when they were only twenty because Danny's mother was pregnant with Danny.

Danny had had this old 1970s era picture of his parents sitting side-by-side on a couch and looking worried, a picture snapped by Danny's grandmother in the moment his parents announced their marriage. In the six months Nadine lived with Danny she often picked up the picture and gazed at it curiously. Danny's grandmother had certainly meant to take a picture of two excited people and gotten a picture of two worried people instead.

Marvin invented a new dance move on the dance floor that night, for Nadine liked to shimmy in circles, and so Marvin would wait for her ass to come broadly beaming, to come a-shake-a-shake-a-shake-shake shaking around, and he'd smack it (kindly) every time.

Marvin waited patiently throughout the afternoon while Nadine worked through four plates at the All-You-Can-Eat buffet. She would fill up on noodles and bread too fast but still, four plates, admirable. "These places are a trap," Nadine would ｇｒｉｐ, 'ｉｆ ｆｒｉｉ ｉｉｒｉｉ ｉｉｆ ｉｆ ｉｉｉ, ｉｉｉｉｉｐｉ ｅｉｒｉｌｊｉｉｉ ｉｉｉｉｉｌ, ｌｌｌ ｌ ｊｌｌｒｌｉｉｉ ｉｉ/ｌｉｉ had never learned one single lesson about overeating, not one lesson not never.

But Marvin was alright. Too bad about Marvin, he was alright. He'd say: "Who doesn't like food? I like food. He likes food. She likes food. They like food. Who doesn't like food? We all like food. Show me the human who doesn't like food and I'll find that human a therapist to help them like food like humans should do. Cuz we all like food. Don't fault yourself for liking food. Especially salty, especially sweet, especially MSG-ridden, especially high fructose corn syrup-pipelined-in-

and-pumped-full food. Especially cheese. Especially, perhaps, falsely delicious per additives that cause death but even still admittedly delicious all the same food. Food is food. We all like food. Don't be too grumpy with yourself for loving so strongly the food that is food that is in of itself food, and its soooooooooooooooo many lovely flavors."

Nadine would have noodles; noodles you could see through sometimes but mostly noodles that had been boiled alive and drained of all water. She would have white bread and rye bread and bread she could chew on one bite of for most of five minutes. She would have small square cakes made of nothing but whipped cream and what was technically cake but was still cream even so. She would eat the fried fish and the fried chicken but only until one year from now when she would go vegan for the planet and vegan for the sake of humanity carrying on and vegan for the sake of animals and vegan for her health. She would eat the macaroni. She would take three bread rolls off the tray of bread rolls which didn't count as neither wheat bread nor white bread but pure deliciousness. She would eat the ice cream from the ice cream dispenser pump thing like at an old timey gas station back in the old days of gas use but only until one year from now when she went vegan etcetera. She would also eat the spaghetti cuz that was also noodles-centric and noodles in general were the nectar. She would always have a heaping spoonful of mayonnaise-intensive, cheese-intensive potato salad until the day came for veganism etcetera. She would eat the small slabs of brownies and the large slabs of cheese, lots and lots and lots and lots and lots of cheese, especially cheese wheels (until vegan etcetera). She would even eat the soups though she considered the soups the most risky part of any buffet cuz anyone can sneeze in a soup if they want and once she even saw someone cup soup out of the buffet's soup tureen with their hand (!!?!) back in her childhood, that someone just cupping their hand down into the soup tureen like they were hunkered down at a branch of the Brazos River back there in the Wild West, and then lifting back out the hand and lapping up cream of mushroom soup straight and right out of their palm. Anyway, she saw that happen once. And anyway, Nadine would eat the slabs of ham (until vegan etc.) back in those days, or in right now anyway these days of all-you-can-eat buffets that were such a trap cuz she would eat until full and then eat until sick. She wondered why cannibals didn't set up food buffets to catch live food coming out of the food buffets all too full up and so sluggish and so sleepy and so easily catch-able with, like, a butterfly net.

Nadine lost a pen in the public toilet, in the toilet itself. There was no way she was going to reach in and retrieve the pen, but she looked down at it interestedly, for it had once been in her hand and been her pen and now it was lost to fate.

Nadine drank from every other drink on the table.

Nadine was finally one day struck by lightning, in the midst of a mild, perhaps even sullen thunderstorm.

The lightning bolt took her off her feet and then the next thing she found, she was looking up at the growling sky from the field floor. Her own bolt, the bolt in her head, was unbearably hot for a week after, but otherwise she was alright.

Of course, from then on, her life would become a scattered thing, fragments of people and events that could never be strung together as a cohesive whole. But otherwise, the lightning had little effect. Or, anyway, next-to-none.

Nadine had Bedford remove the bolt from her head a few days later because it looked a bit funny and anyway Nadine thought it was highly unlikely she'd ever be so lucky as to be struck by lightning again.

-The End-

Berticia

"He was the first boy I ever let stick his finger in my ear," she would say.

She was a sucker for a Q-tip and an even bigger sucker for fingers stuck in her ear.

She was also the only one brave enough to steal silverware.

From other tables.

In the restaurant, I mean.

Under the eyes of the most evil waiter known thereabouts, no less.

The first thing in the morning is always fear.

Fear of which bad road this day might bring.

You can't so much as wind a car up.

Can't so much as.

Not without bringing down a bottle of pretense.

Or upsetting twice a switched-position hand.

My feet are firm on this plush bath mat.

I only wish as far as thick pillows.

But to the restaurant, to the restaurant we must go, sigh.

The next table in the restaurant is full of dim people.

"Dim" is mean, but that's on them themselves, cuz they themselves seem very, very mean, as well as dim, so.

Later, I'll cut myself on a vending machine over a candy bar.

Find their dimness right there laughing on my shoulder.

Laughing at me.

It's Virginia Woolf at the next table, sans the baby.

She was in a theater play, this Virginia.

Berticia slips over to the next table.

Gets us (me) an extra fork.

To replace the one dropped on the floor.

When I switched the position of my hand.

Not even the dim people at the other table notice nor laugh at me. Whew!

They're too busy faking at being great authors of their fates.

-The End-

Bestest Oldest Sweater You Got

The oldest sweater Sam owned scratched against him, had become more instead of less scratchy over time, and had a hole in the elbow.

Sam was once again contemplating sleeping in a graveyard. Churchyard, that is.

Twas a perfect time to do so.

But then, of course, that might be cursing himself.

But then again, why would it be? He was a harmless sort and meant the least of his harms for those already dead.

Just now the warmth of the fire of the hobo camp is bothering Sam, and he sits dazedly watching the rest of the galaxy of campfires dotted into infinity along the beach.

Nearby, a hobo mother isn't taking care of her hobo children, and the hobo children are, of course, crying. How would you like to watch your mother suck on a small glass pipe all the day through?

Sam expected/worried at any moment one of the hobo children would sit beside him, in that psychic way hobo children have of knowing who might-would-maybe protect them and who wouldn't.

But Sam didn't have the capacity to be a comforting semblance of a rag of a human lump just then. He wasn't refraining from the pipe either just then.

He made sure his Protector Aura, what there was of it, was sucked in tight against him and stuffed away to capacity in his pockets. So as not to draw as if to refuge, draw these hobo children, draw them into any sort of belief that he was any sort of miracle/social worker who could work societal miracles.

Also, if Sam were to point out a small otter struggling against drowning just near the pier, Sam's old Dalmatian would refuse to go to the rescue. Not "refuse," more along the lines of that it wouldn't even think to go to the rescue. Sam's old Dalmatian was named Spot, of course, and was lazy like its name's originality.

Sam would have had to himself rescue the theoretical drowning otter.

The two hobo children, little boy and little girl, drowning in their tears to watch their hobo mother enjoy her pipe all the day through. Though "enjoy" was a strong word.

Sam regards a collection of tri-cornered cement blocks. He reckons it must have taken them, the mysterious, industrious Them, some great wallop of industry to get these cement monstrosities all the way here.

Then Sam kicked at the sand.

Surprised himself by revealing a half-empty salt shaker.

Its lid gone and its threads and edges all worn away by the sea.

Every last found salt shaker was like a ghost of Sam's former addiction to salt.

Well, not just "like" but also "exactly" a ghost.

What's seaside living all about anyway?

Sam wanted to ask one of the hungry faces around the fire.

He thinks how there must be a bench in the churchyard to ￼￼￼￼ ￼￼￼￼ ￼￼￼, ￼￼, ￼￼￼￼￼￼ ￼￼￼ ￼￼￼￼ ￼￼￼￼￼￼￼ ￼￼ churchyard, but anyway. But anyway, no curses from the dead, only blessings for sleeping close by, right? The dead liked their visitors, so said the living.

Right? Sam asks his own answerless depths.

Or so Sam thinks to assure himself for another five minutes. Ten minutes at best.

Dalmatians are the world's laziest dogs, a fact every man, woman, and child should know. Dalmatians are ornamented on fire engines because they don't run around trying to help when a fire engine arrives at a fire, they don't get underfoot, they just sit there indolent, time passing, watching the world go blow in inferno, watching the dancing flames, genetically remembering ancient Dalmatian days wherein their titan Dalmationian-Gargantua ancestors would put out fires by swallowing gallons of water into special stomach sacs and then sit spitting the water at the fires' foundations. But remembering them forlornly because Dalmations nevermore since those cave times could cross fact with purpose.

Sam shifted, stood, moved from his place on the beach train tracks to avoid being hit by the beach train. In case he passed out on the beach instead of passing out in the churchyard on a cold stone bench. He gathered his bottles (all three of them, barely a plural amount of bottles he had to admit, only probably passingly in his possession he had to admit, but he still liked to think of them as "his bottles") and scooted down the sand. Closer to the bonfire so that its appearance against the night sky could inspire him evermore.

Not that the beach train was dangerous. Meant for children as it was. Not that the train ran at this hour. Not that it was really a train but a very small version of a train with dune buggy tires, that sat two children per each of its cars and caboose. Not that it went fast enough to kill, not kill all that much anyway, if it ran you down. But to be fair to the beach train, it did run during the hours Sam slept, wherever he slept. But it always creeped Sam out, sitting on any sort of train tracks whatsoever, even train tracks that were really just tire tracks on soft sand, because of the manner of which his fellow hobos always opted for sleeping their way to suicide in the real world, the cold world beyond the beach fires, the real world of trains where real trains weren't only meant to dolly along a beach at 2 miles per hour.

Yeah, thinks Sam, thinking about how the beach train was meant for children, but not the hobo children, who could never conjure the ten bucks necessary.

Yeah, thinks Sam, thinking how he'd have his sleep in the churchyard that night because of all the potential for dreams.

-The End-

Bet You Bleed

"I bet you bleed with the best of them," said Tuskvarney, thinking for a moment in his newfound wild sense of reality that he was in a movie. Unfortunately, he wasn't in a movie, just in a fistfight with a deer hunter in the parking lot of The Near Bar, which was not just a bar nearby but also "The Near Bar" according to its neon.

But thus, at Tuskvarney's rash declaration, the hitherto somewhat-savage-seeming deer hunter dropped his fists to his knees and laughed long and loud, and then said: "Okay, son, let's knock off this nonsense. Come on in now and we'll have us a shot of tequila and a long tall cold one."

And then the deer hunter's arm was around Tuskvarney's shoulder in a way that said *be my buddy or suffer a broken neck whichever suits you* and then they were moving together toward the bar like the oldest of friends in the way of old friends with one old friend having the other old friend in a pretty substantial headlock, wherein (in the bar, not in the headlock) Tuskvarney had first seen the gallery on the bar wall of framed pictures of deer hunters posing with dead deer, which had been what riled him to fighting mode in the first place. *I'm a pretty damn good vegan, you'll see,* was what Tuskvarney sometimes thought to himself, patted himself on the back about.

Tuskvarney tamped down on his adrenalin flow, but at the same time doubted he could get through an entire beer without making another comment about the pornographic nature of the pictures of the deer hunters posing with dead deer on the bar wall. And then when that happened, when the comment would be made, Tuskvarney'd surely be out in the street again with another deer hunter, Tuskvarney's righteous fists raised, him mistaking reality for a movie once more. And then there'd be some cutthroat moment of speech, of words strung quick-asquip together like a movie line, like a line of dialogue in a movie, once again escaping Tuskvarney's hopelessly chapped lips.

Yeah, a movie line from a violent but boring movie that had long since forgiven Tuskvarney... or no that wasn't it... had long since *given* Tuskvarney the idea he could outfistfight someone (a wrong idea), or anyway a movie from a boring Sunday, a turgidly violent movie screened one Sunday afternoon deep back downward in the high dream lit afternoons of Alaskan childhood wherein you were always indoors watching movies 7 months a year, yea o yea o yea, way deep down backward in the twilight afternoons of his Alaskan childhood, a violent but boring movie that had long since given Tuskvarney the idea that he was cut out for outfistfighting in fistfights, which he wasn't, as was not anyone in the whole wide world, not really.

Everyone's fists up, and some line delivered at the next deer hunter, something ringing like: "If you're such a big man let's see your fists work as good as your gun!"

Something like that. Something like: "Okay, deer hunter extraordinaire, let's see you hunt a victory up against my fat fingers closed against themselves!"

Something like that. Or a line delivered like: "If you, sir, were half the creature that deer you killed was, you wouldn't be drinking yourself to death in a dump like this!"

Or a line such as: "Hey, deer hunter, if you're such a hot shit how come I'm hot shitter?!" Then KAPOW with the fist on that one for punctuation.

Or a line such as: "Hey, if I was a deer hunter such as you, I'd stop deer hunting soon as a vegan such as myself broke both your feeble little trigger fingers!"

Or a line like: "Deer hunter, I'm gonna punch you so hard you're going to be hunting a straw to eat with, instead of a fork!"

Or a line like: "You, sir, may be able to defeat a deer with a high-powered rifle at 8000 yards but why not try these hands of mine crusted into fists instead of hooves for once in your life?!"

Or a line such as: "Hey, deer hunter, I'm gonna punch you so hard that from now on you'll only be able to hunt by the light of the stars!"

Those were just Tuskvarney's first drafts of his next line of dialogue per his next pre-fight warmup utterance toward some poor, beleaguered deer hunter.

Like screenplays for movies come in first drafts, or so Tuskvarney thought maybe.

And the doubt over what the line might be tailed Tuskvarney, as he went back into The Near Bar with his new bestie, as his thoughts tailed off into The Near Bar which was a bar called that because it was near enough for people who drank and was near enough, also, to killing fields.

-The End-

Betsy

Daylight on a busy road. The sun spoke highly. The clouds had all been kneaded like dough, and paired off. Gil's heart was limping. His mind was dialed to a low level of baseless worry. His pet garter snake, Little Loo, was coiled around the upper arc of the steering wheel. The exit for Streator, Illinois, loomed and was gone. Gone so Gil could reckon aloud: "That's a cool name for your town." With no link from words to action, he snatched a black marker from the dashboard. Gil thought of a lady friend. With the marker, and his mediocre drawing skills, and one eye still dutifully on the road, he made a crude copy of her face in the upper left corner of the windshield. He drew a cartoon balloon out from the face. Inside the balloon he wrote: *Deep down I miss you too.* Gil sucked deep on the tart car air. Exhaled the whole of the reserves of his endearment. *Please, my friend,* he asked himself, *why don't you ever just simply forget?* Winter trees were like dead giant spider legs on the roadsides. A cornfield filtered past. The sun twinkled. Reflected angel steps. The pinhead-lurking kinds of angels. And it spoke of wellness (the sun, not the pinhead) while dazzling the scales of wending, winding, spiraled Little Loo.

-The End-

Betty, Firefighter

Betty was all man. Don't get him wrong by his name.

He was a firefighter. He is a firefighter, correction.

He sits at the card table at the back of the firehouse leaning in close to another firefighter saying: "We never sleep. We undo each dawn like fresh red shoes. We'll kiss a kind cat if we see one. We love golden doors. We like it this way. We snitch good manners from those who know better to make ourselves better and then we go on and make the world around us better. If one of us were to see a pigeon at the very top of one of those roofs that goes up in a spire and if that pigeon were all alone then we would take that as evidence of all pigeons having individual personalities and senses of self. We plant a row of vegetables in our flower garden. We hold forth in shyness. We are, by gum, firefighters."

"I agree," says the other firefighter.

With that settled, they looked up to see the kids from the local hospital had arrived. With a little bit of effort, the kids were soon sitting in a circle around Betty. Betty snapped his fingers at the other firefighter, who got Betty's favorite book from its place atop the cabinet full of axes.

Betty cracked open the book and read without preamble:

"**Chuckle the Chitmouse by Elizabeth Fantoma**. Chuckle the Chitmouse chuckling, wirty watching out faceless metal didn't make a sudden clanging move. Metal man carrying maybe a spear. No, Chuckle didn't like that. **Learn to love yourself**, thought Chuckle the Chitmouse. Chuckle kept having the feeling of wanting to be mournful because he was just a mouse but then an internal roasting nut engine grinding gippy him guppy him gum gim gim gim toward just being happy with being a chitmouse actually. Chuckle took a prod thought to the hull of a fat ear that he both should and oughtta investigate that stone spire sticking up between the two lamp poles. **It would be a day's journey but worth it and I'd more as likely not surely find crumbs of cackling cake-cake along the way, me, and why cake of all the crumbs?** Don't know, Chuckle thought, and he never thought aloud, some mice thinking and squeaking their thoughts aloud, but back again. **Why cake crumbs of all crumbs?** Chuckle thought back again. **Because,** Chuckle the Chitmouse answered himself, **I feel it in my toothpick bones. The End."**

The kids from the local hospital stared up at Betty with a row of slightly gaping mouths and eyes reading confusion. Embarrassed, the chaperone ushered the children out of the firehouse and back to the hospital.

Betty returned his attention to the other firefighter, who had produced a deck of cards because he wanted to have another go at solitaire.

"Kids are alright," said Betty, "But trees are better. That's why pretty soon I'm gonna start fighting forest fires and stop saving babies from their stupid cribs."

"Cool," said the other firefighter, whose name, by the way, was Chantelle.

-The End-

Bickee Bickee

Barney was the worst of smokers.

Cuz back then, back then at the ultimate choking end of the age of humanity's tempestuous, eternally unfulfilling affair with cigarette smoking, Barney was the worst of smokers.

But not due to the amount of cigarettes he smoked. For him, daily, it was about a pack-and-a-half. Not so bad. There are some smokers out there, man o man.

Maybe there are people out there who smoke four packs a day, right?

Barney himself had, on one bad day in his bad youth, fumed through an entire carton in less than 24 hours, by hunkering down and plunging ahead and puking his guts out several times and really almost dying. But he was at least a little proud that at 11:48 p.m. on that day, smoking the last of the cigarettes in the carton, he'd lay back into beach sand and thought what he thought was his final, valiant thought: *I love the beach. Everyone should have access to a beach at least once in their life.*

But that whole fool smoking-a-carton-of-cigarettes-in-a-day thing was due on a bet, due on Barney's high school gambling problem. Nowadays, high school was a distant memory of absolute shitheaps and general cruelty (toward Barney, of course, mostly all toward Barney or so he felt or so it seemed), and nowadays Barney had an acceptable average maintained with his pack-and-a-half, so he wasn't the worst of smokers in that way.

Nor was Barney the worst of smokers in that he sneaked his smokes in toilets or away from caring eyes. Nor was he the worst in letting go clouds in people's faces or lighting up where he wasn't supposed to. Nor was he even the worst in clumsiness, dropping cigarettes in his lap or putting holes in the shirts of nearby others. Though he did do those things.

Barney was just the worst in terms of how he just wasn't right for smoking in the worst sort of way. Barney was a mistake in terms of smoking.

Like Barney takes up rolling cigarettes. Barney can roll cigarettes so loosely the tobacco burns right down through the half-assed paper cylinders he builds without the burn so much as touching the papers themselves.

Barney rolls and he rolls, making messes both at home and on his private barroom table of armies of little balls of white, of the many brown-turning tendrils of tobacco. He rolls and rolls, licking with his ragged tongue until the finished product is a sodden and unlightable mess, and Barney rolls and he rolls one end of a ciggy, singing *my ciggy my ciggy when will you be done,* and he flounders rolling the other end, twists and twists to try and make the cigarette true, twists as though he's going to press the tobacco back into a plant and tears the operation in half at the last. He grapples for the pouch to start again, but tips the pouch entirely onto the beer-muddled barroom floor.

Barney thinks now you've dumped it on the floor.

Barney stares down the ruin and a strain of despair that he's made for himself, it crawls in, and he thinks he may never move or flex or walk or twitch again.

He could trace back how this particular strain of despair had begun infecting him sixteen years ago when there were these fourteen days of no parking on his block due to street construction. "No parking on my block for fourteen days!" Barney had wailed into his couch over and over again until the neighbors knocked and checked on him. He had been doing a little cocaine at the time, too, so.

So but then, from then, the despair hung close, ready, just like his coffee cups.

They're just Egyptian coffee cups to other people, but to me they're nostalgic and melancholy and from my childhood, from my grandmother's house, from back when, from back when, from back when I was happier go luckier...

Barney goes back to smoking what is already rolled for him. But he buys too cheap, smokes twigs one day, smokes sandpaper the next. He buys bigger cigarettes, but despite his capacities he can only ever manage to smoke about 70 of a 100. He really gets out his wallet, but an expensive brand puts a nerve-wracking growth on his tongue. "What is that on my tongue?" Barney says in the mirror. He goes to the doctor and is told that he shouldn't smoke, and he will only get more cold sores if he doesn't eat some fruit. Then Barney's in the supermarket with a dozen plastic bags, oranges and bananas and kiwis and artichokes, standing before the cigarette case and fussing through his Pabst Blue Ribbon haze to remember what brand he was trying smoking before attempting rolling. The red kind? The blue kind? The brown kind? That angelic white box? He buys the short tan box, opens it to find cigarettes without filters. Barney audibly gasps. Barney says: "Fuck." But now he's learned about the shorter boxes what he should've known twenty years ago at least. But Barney's throat, with all its wear, isn't steeled against unfiltered cigarettes, and after smoking a pack of them he spends a week gargling salt water and taking medicine meant for asthmatics.

And yeah, Barney is aware of the kids today and their vaping, thanks very much. Don't think he isn't of the cutting edge, don't think Barney isn't hip to the beat of the kids and their kid-ways, don't think Barney isn't aware of these things happening in these modern times. But how, Barney wonders, does vaping even work? Cuz, he wonders, is it electric? Cuz seems like vaping is electrical. Cuz if vaping's electrical, Barney's lips are always too wet for electricity, and he just needs to stick with the paperback cigarettes, the ones from the olden days.

Smoking is expensive. A pack-and-a-half a day costs around six thousand dollars a year. To support this habit what Barney does is, he paints postcards. It's true. It's all he does. It's cute. It's his one note of sweetness. It's like the long ago ladyfriend Barney had so much trouble with, but he still loved the way she turned her wrists out when going to hug him. God, that break-up. He'd fucked that up. That was a day of screaming trauma. Barney had at least one of those days per year. That's why the quiet of the hand-painted postcards. It was the same as whispering your career, Barney always figured. Hand-painted postcards are out there. In quaint little shops. Or Barney worked the hippie fairs. He sat in his booth he had. Sometimes he closed his booth and ambled down to one of the meditation booths and sat under crystal triangles wrapped in copper wires and thought of a boy who walked on a dock that protruded far too scarily far into a deep blue lake under a cloudless star-filled night with a fat full moon, and the boy would be lightly clutching a handful of forget-me-not-sized bells, each tinkling a little, as in: *ding ding ding ding, ding ding ding ding ding, ding ding ding ding ding ding ding ding ding.* That exact and certain number of "dings," that exact amount of a little tinkling of dings.

Barney'd painted *that* postcard, too, in fact. Yeah, fuck yeah he had.

Cuz yeah, a small squadron of postcard painters, out there in the world.

Barney doesn't mind it so much and in fact likes painting postcards oftentimes, though often enough, too, sopping around with those tiny brushes doesn't quite satisfy. "Perhaps... perhaps..." Barney ponders, at home, at times, after putting another cigarette burn in his armchair or drawing a pint of blood trying to clip a tobacco stain out of a fingernail. "Perhaps postcard painting simply isn't destructive enough for poor old me..."

So! In the World Famous Chinook Tavern one lonely, boozy night, Barney was painting a postcard, this one depicting an idyllic scene from a farm. Barney was drunk to where his hands weren't shaking, to where the lines of the fence and the farmhouse and the hayseed with the bucket of slop for the pigs were coming out pretty straight and fine; this work wouldn't number among Barney's impressionist cards. He painted intently and lushly, interrupted on occasion by some woman or another, who would pause in her traces and exclaim and compliment. Barney responded to these fans by baring his hopeless teeth and saying "Yes, yes, thank you," and driving the women instantly away. He was also interrupted when his cigarettes set the tip of a paintbrush afire or burned more hairs off the backs of his hands. Mistakes were being made. The ones involving the women were the hardest. Why could he not commune with the creatures? Barney felt like spooning out his heart because he could not speak to the ladies and make them melt.

Or not even melt. Just talk. Talk to him. Talk to Barney.

And so it was this one lonely, boozy night Barney was wielding cigarettes like an aging Olympic torch bearer setting out flares after getting a concussion and killing an aging Olympic swimmer passenger in an Olympic transport van accident on the interstate, and so thus it was Barney melted a hole in his plastic cup.

The proprietors of the World Famous Chinook Tavern had given Barney a plastic cup filled with water to snuff his cigarettes in as the prize for smashing two ashtrays in the prior week. But Barney lanced this plastic cup with a cigarette, letting loose a puddle of water and turning the plastic cup into a molten thing. And now Barney was at odds as to where to stub his cigarette, moving it drearily around, drunk(!), needing to tap, making tracers, the ash ever-lengthening. Setting the cigarette on the paint set was no good.

He kept his paints nice.

Barney tried tearing the lid off his cigarette pack, to make a sort of prop, to prop the cigarette up, like. Just a vague plan, but something he could do, but in tearing he just tore the pack in half and littered cigarettes everywhere.

Barney had to settle for placing the cigarette on the table, and when burn holes appeared here and there in the wood, he had to settle for balancing the cigarette on the flat side of his prone lighter. The lighter was cheap and plastic, and it wasn't long before the burning cigarette seared into the lighter's hull and a geyser of butane erupted, snuffing and tossing aside the cigarette, showering everything. The geyser spent itself and Barney regarded the mess and then the guilt and paranoia and irrational thoughts came creeping in. Barney wondered if anyone had seen? *My God*, thinks Barney. ***My God and my Goddess, the outcome could've been deadly, if that fiery cigarette had sunk all the way into the lighter and ignited it as a payload!***

Barney shuddered, then picked up the lighter as though it were dynamite. He kept it horizontal, so to not spill; it was slick all over with butane and still half full. It would have to be gotten rid of, but not in the bar. If he gave it to the bartender to throw away, he'd get the boot forever. The proprietors of the World Famous Chinook Tavern really didn't like Barney. If he threw the lighter away himself, in there, in the bar, someone would find it in the garbage can and retrieve it and use it and blow themselves sky high. Flushing it down a toilet was bad for the environment. Barney would have to dispose of the lighter somewhere out-of-doors. So Barney rose, and moved, in his shambling version of sneakiness, in his swimming way, in his glum roll of elbows and knees, moved through the blur with the lighter horizontal twixt thumb and forefinger, moved through a wooden swinging door into the cool night toward the dumpster that stood just inside the alley across the street. He was softly-focused on his objective, he was making

a roundabout target of the dumpster, even though during the
endless slog from the sidewalk to the yellow center line of East
Main there sometimes seemed to be two dumpsters, and once
even three. Why was Barney having so much trouble lifting
his feet? Why was his neck becoming goo and not lending any
support to his head? He was not getting anywhere. He was
too in love with keeping the lighter horizontal. But the lighter
needed to be kept horizontal. Ah! Ahaha! Maybe his cape was
caught! Maybe his cape was caught in the door of the World
Famous Chinook Tavern! Maybe his cape was pulling him
backward. But no. He never wore capes. It was like how when
Barney had this one dream repeat itself. It was a dream where
he was walking on an empty dirt road under a yellow moon he
couldn't look up to see. He was walking in the middle of the
road and couldn't stray toward the roadsides so he was glad
there were no cars. At first, he was singing to himself a song
he'd made up but could never find the rhythm for. *Those coffee
cups aren't important any longer, the bald man who sat at the mouth
of Dunbar Alley ain't there no more neither, and those men you
thought you could bring beer to in the parks so to make friends with
those men, those men aren't there any longer, neither...* went the
song, and so on and so on. Then there was a woman walking
beside him in the dream. She said: "I hate Emily." He said:
"Hatred is unattractive and out-of-fashion. It's the same with
war. War is government-sanctioned murder. Murder means
hatred. So don't say you hate. Get along with people." And the
woman brushed her hair back and sighed and he'd want to kiss
her on her freckled cheek but then he'd think how he was only
dreaming and he'd wake up feeling lonely. But now Barney was
only meant to be getting the dangerous lighter across the street
and the act was fraught with goo. Strange. It wasn't as though
he'd dropped acid. That was high school again. Had there been
a mickey in his whiskey sour? He had enemies and probably

people after him. He decided it would be best to duck his head and get across the street and get the very dangerous explosive lighter into the dumpster so he could get back across the street a second time and protect his postcard paints and paintings before they were destroyed by his enemies.

But a police car glided in front of Barney then, whistling its brakes and blocking the path to the dumpster. A policeman with a cruel face, a features-clipped-out-of-soapstone-with-a-bone-knife-sort-of-face, this policeman slit his eyes and peered out the window at Barney like a cobra peers at a soon-dead rat. Barney, actually, thought he just might die, speaking of which.

"Hey, buddy," said the policeman, pulling a cigarette free from a breast-pocketed packet and popping it between his lips. "Where you off to?"

"I'm sick." Barney's watering eyes slipped across the officer's nametag. It read: Officer Maschmeier. Officer Maschmeier said: "Sick? Yeeeeeah. You sure look like shit alright. You weren't gonna be sick in the street were you?"

"No."

"I said: you weren't gonna be sick in the street were you?"

"No."

"That's a ticket."

"I wasn't."

I II IIIII' jIIII, IIIIIIIIIIII

"I'm not that sick."

The policeman laughed like a devil. Barney's stomach rolled over. The policeman said: "You got a light?"

"No."

"You do so right there in your hand. I could cuff you for being a lying, shit-ass drunk in public."

The cop looked at Barney like a cobra looking at a rat (again, like that!), and Barney being the rat his every joint and juice froze. Then, while Barney did nothing at all, the cop snatched away the lighter, magician-style, nipped it from between Barney's two fingers and then had it in his own hand before Barney could realize, then bent to it, the cop bent to the lighter, poised it just beyond the tip of his cigarette, put his thumb on the wheel. And there was a fireball. There it was. A freakish moment, framed forever in Barney's otherwise shiftless memory. The cop's face and hands and hair and shirt, all of it burst into flame. The smell of burning flesh, a smell Barney had always read about but never actually smelled, flooded into his nostrils and slammed the nostril doors shut behind it and then ran around inside the works of his olfactories, smashing everything. Barney watched the cop yelp and then somewhat slap away the flames with hands like bats and then the cop roiled in his seat panting and shrieking, and Barney had a moment of crushing uncertainty as to how to put this mistake to rights, or whether maybe to not do anything and just stand there in the middle of the road for good, forever still and silent until he was no longer Barney but a heap of decay. But then something moved in Barney. He glanced all around and saw no help at all, but did notice that the streets were adjusting themselves at odd angles, and that his head was flowing backward on his neckline to catch them, and so Barney felt a surge inside him and he pivoted, his shoes scratching the asphalt, and he took a last look at the howling cop to be pretty, pretty, pretty, pretty okay, pretty, pretty, pretty, pretty okay, pretty, pretty, pretty, pretty sure the cop would live, and then Barney went running. As soon as he gained speed there was nothing but his own breath. He had entered a tube, and the tube had no sound, and it shunted him onward with a great inner wind and it spiraled down sidewalks and through alleys and gave him underwater glimpses of streetlights and underwater glimpses of headlights and lastly deposited him into the park, where Barney found that he had unexpectedly waded well into the middle of a duck pond. The water was totally fucking freezing. And now there were only gentle sounds, crickets and sleeping ducks murmuring, and the world was not quaking around Barney. The water was giving him some sense as it soaked through his pants just below the knee. He could take the time to look at his hands. There was that tiny stain on his pinkie. He worried the stain was the sign of a disease. It had been there for months. He had been too worried to mention it to the doctor, at the time of the cold sore visit. Every day Barney worried about the disease causing the stain and every day Barney looked away from his hands. He waded out of the pond.

Other hands appeared then, grabbing him and twisting him down one of the park paths and up against the cinderblock of a park bathroom. The quiet was gone now, in the rough voices ripping the air and all these giant corrugated kids (even though the word "corrugated" didn't quite mean what Barney kinda thought it meant) grimacing and coughing in Barney's face and then one face skipping off the pinwheel of faces and looming in at him and becoming clear. "Hey, fucker," said a dank-eyed, sharp-nosed boy. "Hey, huddled-in-the-lake motherfucker. What're you hidin' from?!"

Barney answered honestly and right away. "I burned up a cop."

The kids' faces changed, filling with wonder. "What the fuck did you say?"

I set fire to a cop.

"No shit? Which cop?" This was a difficult question. Barney could barely recall his own name right then. Which was "Barney." But as Barney peered into the botched corridors of his memory, with its twittering fluorescents and unwaxed floors, a name tag formed before his vision, a mnemonic name tag composed of a foot crushing a potato and a giant spider struggling through a swamp.

"Officer Maschmeier."

"You burned up Officer Maschmeier?"

"I think just his face was burned off."

Then there was the faint beginning of a siren.

The talking kid looked around wildly, then back to Barney. "No shit?"

Then Barney was king. He was led in splendor to the basement of a building under construction and plopped down among dirty mattresses and given a bottle all to himself and as many cigarettes as he could choke down, and then kids were back with Barney's paint set as well as the half-finished postcards, puppy dog-like retrieved from The World Famous Chinook Tavern, and there was much celebrating on into the morning hours, for Officer Maschmeier had been a nemesis, hated by every heart of every delinquent in that hole, and the reign of terror wrought by his cutting handcuffs and his rabid nightstick was over and gone, and so there was much backslapping and bear-hugging and kids bounding along the walls and Barney the epicenter, him plied with liquors and funny cigarettes that mistook him right up into the air so that he thought singsong thoughts like *gonna get a best friend and treat him right* plus *gonna be in bed earlier each night* and he gazed from above upon the malicious glee that he had brought to pass, and knew that soon he would walk back and offer his wrists and disappear down some black barred hallway to really get in on the cigarette trade, but just now there was a can of spray paint in his hand, and he had the wall to himself and was spraying in cursive over and over **smoke baby smoke baby smoke baby smoke baby** and there was this voice in his ear, this angel voice, so, so sweet, the voice of a woman he'd never know or see or who wasn't even real the way people think of real, her voice wending through his cobwebs and whispering around his ears and mixing what he was spraying with what it was sounding so that in a lovely confusion what Barney could hear in dulcet female notes was: *it's okay, Barney.*

No...for reals. He could hear it.
It's okay, Barney.
It's okay, Barney.
It's okay, Barney.
It's okay.

-The End-

Big Tom

Big Tom, he's the one who makes tomato juice for all of Sussex.

A man with hair all over his body, every inch, more or less fair hair, more a bear than a man hair, though almost never on his head.

Big Tom found it a bit awkward, driving his terrier car around the countryside on the narrowest of roads, delivering bottles of tomato juice like fine Stevensons.

His car was a terrier, a real show dog. It jumped.

He took careful note of each golden hill. Sussex didn't have many golden hills, most of them rather green, but if you caught them just right, between holidays, between rainy days, a certain season, a certain light, just the right sunset, then okay.

His flight had been a weary one.

Big Tom stood in the store watching the cashier agog while the cashier proclaimed to Big Tom that Big Tom opening the can of beer was tantamount to Big Tom leaving the store. Big Tom had indeed opened a can of beer but only because he thought he was a friend to the cashier because of all the smiles they both had been doing hitherto. Using that word "tantamount"?! And when Big Tom had thought he and the cashier were moreso friends?! "Friends," on this, his fourth delivery of tomato juice!

Big Tom had thought the cashier was his friend. He did. He had thought that. He had thought for sure the cashier was his friend.

But then the cashier turned on him with scolding eyes and Big Tom can't bear to be scolded as an adult.

Big Tom is NOT the cashier's friend any longer.

But...? Was he never?

Big Tom finds seagulls generally noisy.

One day Big Tom ran out of tomato juice entirely.

He'd made his biggest batch yet and driven it all over Sussex and now it was all sold and no more tomatoes.

But he realized then he at last wasn't transporting nothing at all, nothing besides himself and a wallet full of money, so he switched out the car for a bicycle, and Big Tom has been happy ever since. He got his bicycle to America by solar-powered freight and headed directly west to where he knew there were hills that were more golden than gold was golden.

Yes, sure, his shoes come apart or else he just loses their inside linings, but still.

Big Tom's *Picture Book Depicting Golden Hills In California* is being released to bookstores next August from John Hunt Publishing and Roundfire Books.

It is a spectacular catalog of golden hills, cast gold by the sun itself. Golden hills in many different shapes and sizes and lays of land.

-The End-

Bigger Than a Tennis Ball

Got several boxes of birthday gifts for my birthday a month after my birthday. Didn't know what the gifts were beyond (inside) their wrappings. Also didn't know who the gifts were from, who, what, where the gifts were from. Return addresses were towns in the U.S. and France I had never heard of and the people had names like Steve Anne. Names I didn't know. STEVE ANNE, STEVE ANNE, I sat there repeating aloud to myself in all capital letters in the space between my mind and my mouth before opening the gifts. STEVE ANNE, STEVE ANNE. And how disappointing they all were, mundane gifts except for one, but largely mundane. Someone called Marcy Chad had sent me a pile of white undershirts, someone named Cedric Jane had sent me a toaster. It was all stuff I didn't much need or even want to love anyone for. Except for this one small lamp. No bigger than a tennis ball. I know that's not the same relative shape but we're just talking size, okay? I waited for dark and plugged the lamp in and the glow it cast was grainy and warm and the kind of thing you could get behind if you were feeling nostalgic for a tiny lamp era that had never been. The return address on that package was some town in either Alabama or Arkansas, for both the town and state abbreviation were illegible. And the sender's name was Madeline Mark, either that or Mark Madeline. Sometimes it's the last name first with some people.

-The End-

Biker Boy

They got the kid addicted to doing laps around the asphalt triangle in the park. Round the kid would go, on his blue and yellow and brave bicycle. Growing up to be a racing man someday, thought his dad. But then the kid went out without his dad one day, with his nanny instead, and took a spill. The nanny just kept reading her book while the kid bent over gymnastically and wept into his Kermit the Frog sneakers.

The dad couldn't explain the listlessness toward laps-around-the-park the kid had from that day forth. The laps had changed from a joy to a chore for the poor kid. Eventually, the dad lost interest, the kid lost interest, and the nanny began taking the kid to the playground instead. There the kid got addicted to looking up girls' skirts. Instead of a racing man, he would someday grow to be simply racy. And being racy was nothing profound. Ahhhhhhhhhh, these simple failures...

-The End-

Biker Man

They would get to the pub at midday on their two forlorn bikes that both looked to be from World War II and were coincidentally built like tanks.

She'd sit in there in the pub with him.

He drank himself to sleep by two.

She would twist his torso and lay him sideways, make his body a hook.

The bartender would put up with it for a while and then come over and tell her to get him to wake up. After the bartender was gone, she'd murmur to him to wake up before the police came. He would sit up but then his head would flop over sideways and he'd be back asleep that way, like a jumble of steel-toed boots piled in a pile, their steel bits bored to nothing from overuse.

Horse racing was silent on the big television, horses going around and around. She'd wait and drink her drink and play in her mind, murmuring bets.

He'd grown up to be a racy man, and gotten her pregnant when they were both in tenth form, and then they'd married and she'd miscarried and but then they were still married. A loveless life stretched out ahead of both of them but then they gradually fell in love even so, deeper and ever deeper in love, and in love with each other's faults especially. He'd sleep in the pub, she wouldn't ever clean the kitchen but once a month, and so on.

He couldn't figure out why he was always so sleepy. He wondered if he'd hit his head once that he didn't remember, because he was very nearly absolutely positive he hadn't hit it falling off the back of his cousin's moped that one time.

He'd expected to have things sorted out by now. But he was working for someone else and always at someone else's mercy.

She'd defend him in the pubs. The bartender would come over a second time and say something and then leave and she'd call the bartender a bastard as soon as he turned his back. She'd also tell the bartender in defense: "I'm waking him up gently."

But in a world where horse racing persisted, being gentle was nothing profound.

Ahhhhhhhhh, these subtle successes...

-The End-

Black Eyed Nontaine

Nontaine's got a black eye she keeps in her pocket.

She pastes it on when she needs sympathy.

Or when she needs you to not listen to what she's saying.

When she needs you to try not to stare at the paste-on black eye.

That's how far her fibs can roll.

Once Nontaine came up to me when I was working at the multiplex.

How I hated the music between the movies.

The Muzak only had a handful of three or four songs that were hits at a given time and they'd play those three or four hit songs after those same three or four hit songs after those same three or four hit songs and those same three or four hit songs and those same three or four hit songs after those same three or four hit songs in a row after a row after a row while you're sweeping up popcorn which has not made the journey from popcorn bucket to mouth what with the slobs moviegoers have become ever since the darkness of the theaters made them collectively decide to not eat popcorn politely, not that popcorn existed before movies except for with Native Americans. And you're in there sweeping up popcorn by the ditties of those same three or four hit songs, you're in there sweeping up popcorn by the ditties of those same three or four hit songs, you're in there sweeping up popcorn by the ditties of those same three or four hit songs, you're in there sweeping up popcorn by the ditties of those same three or four hit songs.

Worse yet... and I'm glad you don't mind me complaining, thanks for the listen... I was still working there three years later when they replaced the songs on the Muzak with commercials. Commercials playing out on the screen before the movie. Advertising abhors a vacuum and back when the moviegoers were just sitting there in the theater, just sat there waiting for the movies, with advertisers just sitting there, too, but the advertisers sitting there burning up their ulcers knowing full well the other moviegoers, their hapless fellow moviegoers blissfully unaware of the power of advertising, could be inhaling worthwhile commercials instead of red curtains and the way those red curtains hung there, concealing great mystery.

Then there came the one day, at last, where there were commercials before movies, and a few stray voices protested but then soon enough the commercials got acquiesced to.

Someday they'll stick commercials inside the movies, and a few stray voices etcetera and then you'll have commercials in the movies, every 10 or 15 or 20 minutes.

So once Nontaine comes up to me and whispers with her lying black eye gone wild and pasted on hastily, pasted on off-kilter so it looks like she got a black eye with a slightly off-set, off-radialed collection of blood vessels bursting.

She whispers: "There's a man out around the back of the movie theater."

She was at some movie at the time with some boyfriend or another who'd taken a sock at her eye, or so she wanted you to think because remember her black eye was a paste on, but I guess I'm just stupidly terrified to get involved on those levels of humanity because though I pride myself on not being evil, I'm also not a hero, much as I hate myself for that, too, as well as hating myself for the usual reasons. You'd think Nontaine was gathering enough bad karma versus her direction in the bank job that someday she'd change it all in for a moreso of a do-nothing job at the top of a skyscraper, or maybe even change it all in for a swift recoup of her youth.

Of course, I had to go check for a man at the back of the movie theater even if I knew Nontaine was a liar. Even if I knew I was no hero who could handle such things. We kept all the brokedown cardboard boxes back there, all the used popcorn buckets and all the ant-cleansed, dried out soda cups back there, and one wrong matchstick from one lost addict would've got the whole building gone up and because there were no exits we'd all have died, or anyway there were exits but they were full of brokedown cardboard that the manager hoarded in the exit hallways because he was afraid of the day we'd run out of cardboard, he was afraid of "The Day It'll All Go Down" as he called it. And anyway, movies melt easy, even on DVD or Blu-Ray they melt easy, even seen in a stream of themselves in a festival movies melt easy. Plus, you would have those same popcorn slobs complaining about their own deaths if there were a fire.

There was no man back there, though, just some stray thought of Nontaine's that changed from a shadow man in her past to some flip fib she had to come tell me so I'd waste a good ten minutes I could have better used snatching a watch of some luckless movie scene forced to show itself to me despite being disconnected from the rest of its movie.

Later in the day, though, I accused her of fibbing and Nontaine took her black eye back out of her pocket and showed it to me guiltily as the only armor she had against the world and it made me suddenly so infinitely deflated and so infinitely sad and I said sorry for being mad at her for her just being Nontaine, such as Nontaine was, and then I said a thousand sorries for my generalized anger and I've been sorry ever since then, really, come to think of it.

For that matter, I'm sorry now. I didn't mean to go too far with italicizing and bolding and underlining my words, if I've ever done that here, or even when I bespoke them in real life. I didn't mean to ever get to the point of enhancing too many words with adverbs. I'm truly very sorry. Nevermore the overdoing of anything, nevermore.

Sorry, sorry, quiet now.

Just watch the movie.

Lift my hand half an inch from where it sits hoping on the thigh portion of my jeans.

Move it across airspace like one of those funny dumb claws in one of those machines where you try and make the funny dumb claw pick up a stuffed animal.

Place my hand, so gently, atop Nontaine's hand.

As she sits beside me because thank God it's me she sits beside nowadays.

And, thank you, I pride myself on not being evil.

I've always steered well clear of harm being brought.

Never building weapons of war for money, like. Not never, not me.

Never requiring a black eye, fake or otherwise, of Nontaine.

Here in the dark as she sits beside me, such an angelic presence, here in the dark.

Here in the dark with me so grateful for her being her as she sits beside me.

Here in the dark, her of the magic, her, even as we are both within the magic, here in the dark.

-The End-

Bland

They ordered the food that was meant to be bland.

He switched to the cheese that was meant to be bland.

She read from the book that was meant to be literary.

They took on the day jobs that were meant to be around equipment that was meant to be dangerous.

They took to the trees that were meant to be leafy.

She drove the road that was meant to be off limits.

He scratched his foot's top for the itch meant to be underfoot.

They watched the helicopter fly by that was meant to float by.

They loved the French fries that were meant to be eaten.

He took on the day job that was meant to cause cancer in ways that were meant to be trouble.

Speaking of death...!

The telemarketer rang the phone at the dead woman's house. RING RING, RING RING.

But even if the woman had answered the phone alive, her living voice would've sounded so disinterested as to be dead in reply to the telemarketer's mission.

The letter from Dachbar Minktonton Materials read: "Dear Mr. Horrocks, we will not be able to feature your entry, 'The Corporate Ownership of Santa,' in this year's gingerbread house competition for reasons that should be plainly obvious. Also, we're sending someone to your house. Sincerely, Security."

Mr. Horrocks had often in the past accused Security's judging committee of making safe choices coupled with paranoia, and this year would be no different.

All his research on the roving bands of stroke patients bearing torches, them gathered together who couldn't afford more than one squeeze toy.

It's not every day you call up a fella named "Sixtoe." It's not every day you get picked up on the street by a fella named "Connaught."

People don't hate you, the telemarketer reminds himself. In fact, everyone wants to talk to you for at least a little while.

Some retirees move to Florida and never die. Think about it. They're still there. They don't die these immortal retirees. Everyone else in their retirement communities dies and that's why no one notices they don't die. But they don't.

They vandalized the menu after eating the bland food, correcting the menu's spelling mistakes, and then went through their receipts to figure out who ordered what, like they had all the time in the world for going through receipts and figuring out who ordered what, or all the time in the world for parking their cars in just the right spot, and/or all the time in the world for deciding on what to wear for what weather conditions.

They were the ones who hunted Santa Claus until proving once and for all that he didn't exist.

They were the ones who switched to hunting telemarketers.

They were the ones who pulled on the pants that were meant to look good on the dance floor.

They were the ones who took the jobs in the offices like the one with the tabulation of a whole lot of painted coin thingies that were supposedly to collect coins meant to be exchanged for goods and services.

They were the ones following the few remaining telephone poles a million or so miles to the place where all the telephone poles began.

-The End-

Blood Shadow

By a blood-looking shadow on her face he became convinced she was going to be in a car crash and couldn't let her friends drive her home. Or so he decided later in a deep dark hole of madness, long, long after she was dead, that that was what he did.

Try and go back in time in various ways. Go on. Try it.

Will and the exercise of will and freewill hand-in-hand, these things are movies.

You got a real good test for a woman. She's got to not be shallow, you're right, you're exactly right. Meanwhile, tho, mind those hands, O Romeo.

One dude needs the back door on the bus and BACK DOOR BACK DOOR BACK DOOR BACK DOOR BACK DOOR BACK DOOR BACK DOOR he calls in all capital letters and then a lady pitches in her own shout from a couple of seconds later BACK DOOR BACK DOOR BACK DOOR BACK DOOR BACK DOOR BACK DOOR BACK DOOR and then that lady gets off the bus, too, along with the dude who had already got off the bus just before her.

Then a blessed moment of fresh and newfound silence.

Bus driver calls out ANYBODY ELSE NEED THE BACK DOOR?

Big laugh from the entire bus.

We talk to younger people so they teach us, as well, that steadfast forces change the world and vice versa, how it's about the order in which you move things, and how, on the contrary, everything on that poster is accurate to a T. Except the editor. This is a movie poster we're talking about here. Cuz, yeah, they've got the editor wrong.

That's why here I sit writing on paper in a notebook with a pen because there he sits next table over trapped on a laptop.

It's my last cup.

It tastes like a mouthful of faked greatness.

-The End-

Blurred, Each of Her Fingers

Each of her fingers, blurred through her haze, each had a ring, each ring representing one day of the week, the Wednesday, Tuesday, Saturday rings and so on. Plus, she had three rings representing the first three months on most calendars: January, February, and March. With all these rings she would always know these days and these months, as she knew all about everything, on through the years.

-The End-

Born Motherlover

"I may as well warn them ahead of time," Alexander said aloud to the grainy atmosphere of the Honda the moment he spied the call box.

He pulled the car over, held his breath, gave a blessing, and turned off the motor, and got out of the seatbelt and out the door and went to the call box.

"Hello," he said to the woman who answered. "This is Alexander Rodeohdoe. I am headed toward San Antone. However, my motor keeps missing when I'm in remote places and I don't have one of those portable phones and I used my spare tire a hundred miles ago. I might be needing a lift from someone who knows best so be expecting an emergency call from me from some call box further up the road." He giggled: *hee hee*, but then he added: "No, I'm serious."

"Maybe you'll give a lift instead of getting one," the woman replied primly.

Alexander's eyebrows jumped to his hairline and he made a whistling circle with his mouth, though no whistle strained out.

"Maybe you'll need to be selfless instead of selfish," the woman said.

"Okay," Alexander said. Then he quickly hung up before he could overdo it with the woman and went and got back in the car. He shook his head. "Why'd she say that to me?" he asked the air, which had now gotten so grainy he could pick out each individual molecule. "Aren't I alright?" he asked.

Then he held his breath. He gave a blessing. He turned the key. The car started. He let out his breath and drove on into the comforting smother of night, and soon watched the moon pop up.

***

"And now it's morning in the Honda Hotel," Alexander says, and sits there smoking everything in sight. Wrappers, bits of shoe leather, lint. His leg muscles are tied up from sitting. He would get out and stretch but there are wild dogs everywhere around the car. They lord over this desolate parking lot atop a hill of grass overlooking the sea. There are carrion birds, too, hopping on the rails of temporary fencing. The dogs bark at the birds and sometimes the dogs move quick as cats and catch the birds and devour them. One gray dog with rips in his coat and a milky eye stops to growl at Alexander, and Alexander's thankful he's behind a rolled-up car window. "Go on," Alexander says. "Get outta here." He's worried. But then he reckons he can drive away at any time, provided his car's dead battery manages to miraculously rejuvenate itself.

Alexander looks at how his face huddles in the rearview mirror. As part of the rearview mirror, Alexander joins the rearview mirror in striping out a section of sky. Stripe. Then through the reflection of the back window he sees the view of the ocean he also sees in front of him, and with the troubled hearing Alexander's had since before he was born, he can hear the wild dogs singing in a vicious kind of mutter, low and dirty. They sing:
roving
roving around
looking
for food on the ground
a wrapper
chew wrapper
chew, chew, chew
I'll go anywhere
I'll lift leg
hey, bird
that's my garbage, bird

get to flying
wagging tail
drinking a puddle
good water
hey, kid in the car
come out and taste it
taste good water
come on out
come on out kid doooooooooooooooooooooooooooooorrrrrrrrrrrrrrrr
But Alexander sits in the car and thinks: no way.

***

Back in the night, Alexander turned off on a side road. "Uh oh, disaster," he said, but he let the car rumble down and down anyway, the road showing him the wrong side of a hill, and it was like parachuting into a whirlpool of pine needles, and branches longed to touch the car and sometimes did, and then the road got bumpy and turned into dirt and shredded, losing substance altogether as a road to invading brush and youngster trees. The car's right fender bounced off a stump. Then Alexander arrived at a deserted farmhouse, its wood gray with weather and its roof collapsed. He paused the car for a breather and dust clouded into the headlights' rays. The car impudently stalled. Alexander tried turning the key and pumping the gas pedal, and then he tried hoping, but the car wouldn't start again.

He gave up and leaned back in his seat and looked at how eerie it was that his headlights showed just some of the woods and some of the farmhouse, and around beyond the lights' frayed edges there were dangerous shadows everywhere and, really, at any moment Alexander expected some moaning madman with fierce bloody railroad tracks of stitches across the face and forearms to lurch into the beams with a raised axe. Alexander switched the headlights off. Then thinking he had, come to think of it, seen someone or something, he turned the headlights back on. *A stubby motherlover* stood a few feet back from the car's crumpled hood. Alexander was amazed. He'd heard of motherlovers, but never actually seen one.

***

I don't know, man. Out on a rainy road at eight o'clock at night. Bad brakes on my car. My leg hashed with poison ivy. My eyesight shot because I lost my one contact but I'm still the one driving. The stubby motherlover holding an enormous potted sunflower sitting all proud of himself next to me. What am I to do? I ask him what he wants.

"I want to take you where we farm these babies," the stubby motherlover says, nodding at the sunflower.

"But why?" I ask.

"Because. It's beautiful there," says the stubby motherlover. "And who doesn't want to at least visit someplace beautiful?"

"Yeah?" I ask, then I ask, my voice breaking: "You got waterfalls there?"

"We sure do."

A silence between us. In the silence, I get misty-eyed thinking about those waterfalls.

"No need for tears. You just drive on along," the stubby motherlover says gently.

We go driving along, me sniffling. But not sniffling so much that I can't stay on the lookout for even just a few additional interesting friends.

***

Some 270 miles later the stubby motherlover says:

"Careful of Officer William Lawrence Stevenson."

They'd planted the sunflower at the border, so the stubby motherlover was only left with a plastic striped straw to hold, and he toyed with that, winding it around and around and around and around and around and around the fifteen or so tiny fingers he had on each hand.

"Who's that?" asked Alexander. Policemen got him jumpier than any old average rabid-looking badasses hanging out in front of any average convenience store, and police cars made him more nervous than behemoth trucks that roared up behind and then roared past showing off the florescent mud the trucks garnered from being monstrous enough to drive through toxic swamps. Yes, but point being the police make me so nervous and I wonder why that is since I've never ever broken any of... well... haven't broken any of the laws of mankind, anyway, thought Alexander.

"Officer William Lawrence Stevenson, he's a highway patrolman along this way," said the stubby motherlover. "He gets into busy nights terrorizing this section of the freeway, especially when a woman friend has just dumped him, and he's both so handsome and so mean that he's always getting woman friends and then always getting dumped. But just obey the speed limit and don't go swerving the way you sometimes יִיִּ־₪₪ ₪₪₪₪ ₪₪₪₪, ₪₪₪ ₪₪₪₪₪₪₪₪ ₪₪₪ I'll let you know when things are okay again."

"Agreed," said Alexander, shaking his head at the thought of a mean cop.

The stubby motherlover read Alexander's mind.

"Yes, yes, the police of your world. One would imagine if there must indeed be police then the ones who wanted to be police would need to pass some sort of test of their instincts for truly being good people."

"One would imagine," said Alexander, and the car kept on through the tunnel of night.

***

270 miles later a tumbleweed came wobbling out into the road and Alexander was forced to run it down. It disappeared under the car without a sound. There was no sound either from some mushroom clouds lighting up the most distant places on the horizon. The stubby motherlover only once pontificated.

"Lookee there, atomic war, never a good idea, same as war itself, never, never, no matter what they might say, never ever, ever, ever, ever, ever, ever, ever, ever, ever a good idea."

***

And 270 miles after that they had to stop for gas in a gas station that they first saw on a hilltop like a crashed spacecraft, and when Alexander climbed out of the car and walked around the front, he had to admire that the tumbleweed was still stuck to the bottom of the grille.

"Holy cow," said Alexander.

"That reminds me," said the stubby motherlover, popping his head out the window. "Of a song."

"Oh sure," said Alexander, uncertain.

The stubby motherlover sang, his voice echoing into the canopy of the gas station pumps.

"The hand that you hold
Will follow the mold
Of every other hand
That you've ever held
And the hand on your heart
Is your own at the start
But cling to the hope
That she'll be your bell!"

The stubby motherlover grinned. "I think I stole the tune."

"I like it," said Alexander.

The stubby motherlover shrugged and ducked back into the car. Alexander glanced over his shoulder at the line of cars stretched all the way down the exit ramp and nervously toot-toot-tooting for him to pump some gas and said again: "Holy cow."

***

"You got a lot of clothes in the backseat," said the stubby motherlover, 270 miles later.

"I live in a studio apartment with only one closet and could only put half my clothes in there so my backseat is the other half of my wardrobe," Alexander said.

"Don't worry about that apartment no more," said the stubby motherlover. "Once you see my country, you won't wanna go back."

***

270 miles later we sat quiet in the car with the dawn coming up behind us. The stubby motherlover had ripped open a teabag of raspberry tea, and emptied the contents of the bag into a cigarette paper, and rolled a cigarette, and was now smoking it. He remarks

"Take, for example, those pillars, which are made of stone and look good against the snow."

"Yeah," I said. The pillars, of Grecian design, blipped along at the roadside, their feet buried in the snow. The raspberry tea cigarette smelled alright. I was waiting for my nausea to subside so I could maintain my driving streak in a good way. Somehow, when I stayed up driving all night and saw the dawn, I always got so nauseous.

***

There it was again, the flutter of plastic near the car's front wheel worrying Alexander. He ate some more potato chips. He was glad he'd stopped to buy more food stuffs. For today he'd eaten eggs and turkey and ham and bread and rock candy. The lady at the souvenir store said it was likely the last time he'd ever even see rock candy and Alexander couldn't pass that up. The stubby motherlover ate nothing, but occasionally stuck out his wide tongue and sneezed into it, and Alexander never watched what happened after that.

The strange new snow was making a universe of itself. Alexander looked at the two bags of garbage on the passenger side floor just below the small feet stuck on the stubby ends of the stubby legs of the stubby motherlover.

"Don't you worry about a little green glowing snow," said the stubby motherlover.

Alexander didn't say anything, but even seemed worried about the two bags of garbage that couldn't be consolidated one into the other because each was equally full.

"Too bad about this oncoming night though," said the stubby motherlover. "We always seem to be coming up on state parks just after dark. But then, even then, the rocks they got in these places do look something special against the light of your world's sun just after it's set itself."

***

Out in the desert, 270 miles later, the stubby motherlover woke up after being curled asleep for seven hours leaving poor me alone with the bunch of papers and notebooks and overstuffed boxes of my thoughts.

"This is the desert," he says, blinking, and smacking his mouth. "The place I'm taking you to is only a little further. Did you pass a big gambling town?"

I nod, then say uselessly: "Yeah."

"Once I found out that those from the town bury their bad guys out here in this very desert. Another slice of that tenacious aggression humankind's always got going."

"That stuff makes me glum," I say.

"It's okay," says the stubby motherlover. "Very soon now your whole world, with a great collective sigh, like all the hummingbirds in an entire nation learning simultaneously to open milk bottle caps, your whole world will at once be tired of killing itself. The addiction to murder of all kinds and the addiction to suicide of all shapes and sizes and especially the addiction to war will end and the entirety of humanity will give their addictive force to all the funtime addictions. Art, drugs, science, religion, sports, gardening, learning, robotics, sex, building, those types of things. Those things will be funtime addictions without warlovers and moneylovers to make them activities to retreat to instead of enjoy. Trust me. Very soon now. People will become puzzled at themselves for fighting for land or prominence. Above all, no more war. I promise."

We're wheeling past telephone poles now, our conversation much longer than it seemed because the sun had gone from its 11 a.m. position where it'd woken the stubby motherlover to now hovering over the western hills.

"They say the sun's yellow but it's white in the desert, I've seen it blackly with my own baby blues," says the stubby motherlover, and laughs.

They flew into the night and, inside, the car felt more like a plane, and in the lines of light from the occasional lightpoles, the stubby motherlover resembled to Alexander a watercolor painting in the passenger seat. There were still cars that they were passing but mostly the cars were going very slow and had their headlights off and were wrapped in their own small shadows, and then a lot of the rest of the cars were faltering and had their headlights dimming or flickering, but, boy o boy o boy o boy, Alexander's Honda...

Well, all I can say is thank God and the Goddess for my copilot, thought Alexander, and though he hadn't ever before cared to make the car speed due to safety reasons, now he pushed the gas pedal down as far as it would go. Alexander was hoping, like a little kid, to get to the front of the entire line of cars. *Oh, these things the mind likes to chew on that have no bearing on the present,* Alexander thought sadly, thinking of how he'd argued with his father in the downstairs den when his father was just confused and couldn't help it because of his brain gone wrong. *Damn me. Damn me. That I'm even driving right now is spectacular as I have no talent for it, I'm nothing at all to this world because I'm nothing more than this world was,* **I think, glancing at the stubby motherlover, who doesn't seem to mind the occasional swerve nowadays but then that had to do, too, with the wobble of the air around the car at this incredible speed, so I reckoned I couldn't always keep being down on myself over every little thing.** Alexander would sit there in the chair by the nook telling his true love how if things were different, they could keep it simple. She'd just cried. *Damn me, I'm not any good,* **I think.** "We made a toy boat with a cage, a raft with rails, me and my dad, downstairs on the workbench, and I really truly didn't guess he was gonna someday die," Alexander said quickly. But the stubby motherlover's thoughts were elsewhere. **I wondered if I could come back someday and get my mom from her refuge in the country, but then again it looked like most anything could be arranged. Something loomed in the road ahead and I gasped, because it was a hangar door, a sun-sized light, an ocean window that didn't belong to any part of anything,** and it was about to devour us and devour the car the same way it was already devouring the road ahead.

And Alexander heard just a small, quick sound when it did, like: *pop*.

-The End-

Bowness

First, maybe a whiff of a giggle here: the town is called Bowness, but not the !!BONUS!! you're thinking of, more a sort of of-ness of a bow in the hair or an arrow in the bow.

Stevens is there, and he ambles today between the laundry and the coffee counter, and every time he leaves the coffee counter, the redhead's eyes tie in his direction. Stevens doesn't notice, and the romance dies the next hour.

Bub is at the coffee counter, too, watching Stevens think and wondering about how Stevens finds so much to think. Bub doesn't have much to think. Bub is just there over breakfast with a grubbed fistful of tea, he's not bothered even by the door he's got to install today, though he's never installed a door with an arching top, this'll be the first time.

Stevens, anyway, looks bothered. Looks to be having an ordeal tussling with his laundry.

Man, it's only laundry, Bub murmurs in a psychic murmur, aimed toward Stevens.

Outside down the end of the street is Brown's Field, where Brown housekeeps a handy wheel, where Brown's cow likes to stand itself against the sky. Knows it looks good against the sky. And Brown's cow must know because it's always perching on a particular hillock that throws it up in bold silhouette no matter the weather, no matter the position of the sun. Brown's cow looks lordly down on the farm, the farm being called The Row, and Brown's cow thinks, in simple cow fashion, about how the farm must be called The Row because it's where things are always being lined up.

Stevens pauses mid-street, exactly central between the door of the laundry and the door of the coffee counter. He regards the cow in its silhouette finery. Something about the simplicity of Brown's cow looking like that checks Stevens in his worry.

He must get over his hatred of laundry. It's only the laundry after all. It's got ancient ritual to it, anyhow. He must enjoy that people have probably been doing laundry for centuries at this point. He should enjoy the ancient feel of the laundry doings in his very genes and bones. Or anyway: it's only laundry.

Cued, a thought slips into Stevens' head, a thought in another voice other than his own, a gruff voice crackling with cigarettes, saying straight to Stevens, taking Stevens by both shoulders and saying straight to Stevens' heart: *Man! It's only laundry!*

-The End-

Boxer G

Gerald Gerard was a professional boxer and would box as much as possible, each and every single day.

This led him to challenge folks he met on the street, to challenge greengrocers, to challenge police, to challenge little kids.

Gerald Gerard never won, except for the fights with children.

Backspear!

Little by little the bedwetting stopped.

First, tho, it ceased altogether.

And then, for good measure, the bedwetting stopped.

The kids were scared to the point of being something more than scared. Even tho Gerald Gerard was human and not, for example, a monster with immense teeth.

You would think, fright-wise, the bedwetting would've surged instead of stopped. But the kids were something more than scared. So the bedwetting stopped.

You would've thought the bedwetting would've started, though. You would think there would've been a dream-drugged feverish fever pitch of a forest fire burning fury of bedwetting. But the hills were dark and the clouds were ominous and the kids were more scared than they had ever been, for whatever reason, like who knows because they were kids, cuz Gerald Gerard was just a man and not a monster, but maybe they were being raised with a healthy fear of fisticuffs. But whatever the case the kids were so scared that their stomachs dropped into their socks and their bedwetting stopped altogether. Lo and behold, the bedwetting stopped.

Admittedly, it was enough for some certain parents in charge of the household laundry to conjecture that all that abject fear had its upside.

"Scoop of flesh with your vanilla ice cream?" the kids asked each other nervously.

Backspear!

Gerald Gerard terrorized these kids, really.

Went to jail for it eventually.

No good that sort of behavior.

Even if you've got aspirations of professionalism in the world of boxing.

Especially if you've got aspirations of professionalism.

-The End-

Breakfast, Thanks, Dana

Elda sat there crying all her tears into her breakfast, and some tears went down her chin and wet the front of her shirt. Her boyfriend had left her but what was making her cry hardest was the ring of dancing blue butterflies round her wrist.

The car was in the parking lot too awfully high above the beach. Elda was having trouble with the very fact she was even breathing.

Down on the beach, far enough away that the fella was ornament-sized, was a fella with a flashlight, poking his finger of a beam on the wave tops and across the sand and against his dog.

Elda waited for more waves to come in.

"Man, that Reena Roberts, she's such a good friend of mine it's tough not to always think of her as my enemy," she said aloud.

She watched a dying fish flop on the pavement beside the car. She hadn't noticed it before. But obviously a wave had hurled it all the way to the cliff top to land right there, smack beside the car.

"Poor fish," she said. "How'd you get so far from home?"

She was aware she was asking a question she already knew the answer to and twas a wave had hurled the fish all the way to the cliff top to land right there, smack beside the car.

Elda thought of leaping out of the car and snatching up the fish and tucking it beneath her arm and running madly around in circles until she found an entrance to the beach path in amongst the shrubbery and then sprinting down to the beach, dirt flying, high heels flying off, running so fast as to fall forward but still at a run, fish tucked under arm all the while, and then reaching the sand and plunging the sand with her size 9 bare feet and being frustrated by the slow bit of sand plunging but then reaching the firm wet bit and finally hurling the fish into the ocean and back to safety.

But then the fish simply died. There on the pavement. The rescue never occurred cuz of Elda's hesitation.

She watched the casino lights wink in the town down the beach.

She said: "I could've picked a more fun town, though. I seem to be the only one having any fun."

Living in her great green satrapy, Elda will sometimes try and catch a sneeze in her hand no matter how bad the catch might be. Once there was a gut in one sneeze, and plenty of times there was blood.

The other Eldas all laugh at her boring and ugly straight brown hair. She's got no imagination with hair. "Do something to raise yourself from ugliness!" the girls catcall.

But outside the satrapy the world is choking and dying from lack of greenery, so Elda doesn't care what the other Eldas think.

Before 11 p.m. free entry was the deal, plus she got £1 vodka drinks. She wondered what the pound sign converted to in Bangkok.

She was the only one in the club. Mindless music, dumb-colored lights smashing, nothing fabulous, nothing explosive. Elda made a joke with herself, laughed, then sat there analyzing why the joke was so funny.

In the depths of the club just past the fog was a creature of a teenager with no hair, big ears, boggy eyes, scars, spots, stitches across his neck where tattoos didn't seem to leave room for stitches, one befogged eyelid thick with mucus, hair gone brittle gray in his twenties, saying to his tired girlfriend: "I'm not a monster, you know."

Inside now were giants on the dance floor. They crushed their opponents and partners both but still somehow had biceps to be admired and not feared.

Elda used chivalry on a corner of the wall. She couldn't wait for her English Breakfast. Especially the sausage. She wondered what it was made from. Later it would repel her, and she'd take up only vegetables.

She had a thing stuck in her ear allowing instant communication.

There was the great dark stretching mystery ocean always within easy sight below a bit of star-packed sky.

Next door was a club with "no juice," as the bouncer would tell you in sullen tones. Dirty white cushions, dirty white fake buttons on the wall, some young drunk with two birds trying to muster energy dancing to the din underwater.

"What're doggers?" he asked her over breakfast.

"They are people who have sex in cars but they say they're walking dogs," Elda informed him.

"Go back and explain that to me logically," he said.

She let a dog crawl in her stomach. For safety. The dog's still there.

A world away dead-eyed men in hoods walked through a red-tree landscape.

There was a cold corporate hotel in the middle of the waste.

Speaking of dead, Elda knows there's a businessman frozen to the pavement outside.

She remembered how when she was a kid, she thought hurricanes were cool. She thought maybe them that didn't want to bother saving people from hurricanes just are like kids and still think hurricanes are kinda cool even though they should know better as grownups.

But she had been there anyhow. She stood drenched in rain, her mouth hanging open. The very city, as far as she could see, shredded and was carried into a suddenly heavenly sunny sky.

"There goes some potted plants," she'd said aloud, trying to pick small details.

"There goes a roasted turkey! There goes an antique chair!"

Finally, the world figured out what would be best and just gave all the moneygrubbing, wargrubbing suits some guns and sent them to an island. All those politicians who liked war so much. A terrific end, certainly. And after that the world got on with the business of peace and Elda watched happily and listened to the world's new heartbeat and the world's new lung drums.

She murmured: "Do not follow; there is no leader."

Just when one would think the fireworks were gonna quit, they'd keep going. Ever since world peace had been declared and nobody had to do anything and they needed to use up all the leftover gunpowder from all the wars that would never happen and besides they got to see fireworks most every night. Because fireworks were ultimately mediocre entertainment but still fun but as long as you just had to realize their exact configurations in the skies would pass from memory so quickly and maybe that was the point, the moments, each moment gratified then gone, and thinking that Elda then carried on with life stumping for and even cheerleading for the greatness of fireworks instead of not, just that the sound of them could use some work so that they made the sound of joy bursting instead of bombs bursting, eh what?

So, Elda sat in the car on the beach and watched some fireworks pop off and seem to bounce their sparks against the stars in the sky.

At breakfast the next morning Elda was crying but luckily only because she had a violent hangover and not because she'd lost another boyfriend.

"At least the bad feelings from the hangover will only last a few hours," Elda thought, spitting away a tear that was fussing on her lower lip same as a butterfly.

"At least it's not a man I need," she thought. "It's just love. Just that. And love, hey. Cuz I can love an animal. Fact is, I can even love a fish."

-The End-

Breakout Brakanza

Brakanza came back to his small home-town town after some several piles of collections of months away in the big foreign city foreign-land-wise.

The tea shop owner in the small-town tea house didn't want to hear about the big city.

The bread shop girl in the small-town bread shop didn't want to hear about the big city.

The lady in the dry cleaners in the small-town laundromat didn't want to hear about the big city.

In Joey's Tavern they were laughing because the pay phone was ringing.

RING went the pay phone.

A call from the last century.

They laughed and they laughed and they stayed slugs at the bar. They couldn't stop laughing. Every time the phone rang. It would stop for a while and then, apparently, the mystery caller would drop another quarter on his end and give it another try and BRRING BRRRING BRRRING BRRING and they couldn't stop laughing.

Brakanza tried to settle on his barstool. He tried to. The legs were uneven way aways down there. The stool and Brakanza tipped, briefly, back and forth. It was almost like having a beer on a yacht. Almost.

Pshaw. His barstool wasn't going anywhere near the Caribbean.

FOUND: PET BUNNY.

Oh, Jesus, in this weather, thought Brakanza.

The hooded dogs place themselves three in a row behind the low wall and the rusted-by-design fence.

Three actresses off to their audition in Brakanza's memory of the big city, one checking a mirror, one checking hair, one staring straight ahead into future fame or anyway future frames with little squares rowed alongside.

Brakanza huddled against an icy wind with all the beers from Joey's girding him. He was enjoying his lonely hilltop bench now.

That had been such a good laugh they'd all had in the bar, Republicans laughing alongside Democrats. Republicans and Democrats laughing alike.

Every time that goddamn shrill payphone rang with that call from the last century.

No one ever answered it, and it went on ringing as funny as fuck.

An event Brakanza had been in just the right time, place, and mood for, and it would never ever stop being funny.

But just now Brakanza watched the sky rip open with snow.

Snow piled on everything in the small town, made the small town look inviting and peaceful instead of grumpy that there were bigger, more holistic towns elsewhere, with much more to do to pass the lifetimes therein.

The lady at the small town's historical society's admission counter didn't want to hear about the big city either.

-The End-

Broken Things

Lots of things are broken right now.

The long hair, the sunglasses, the ever-changing trick seal by his side.

Man imports a massive rage harboring four parrots onto the bus.

Did I say "rage"? I meant "cage."

Man imports a massive cage tall as him, tall as me, four parrots therein keeping their balance. Wheels on the cage and so on. Perches. Feeders. Mirrors for the parrots to preen in. The whole shebang. Parrots living and breathing. Man imports the entire cage contraption rigmarole operation aboard the bus.

Man elaborately ties the parrot cage all down and all secured with bungee straps.

This tie-down-securing mission takes a full three minutes by my watch.

Man unshoulders his duffle bag, kicks the bag under a seat.

Leaves the birds for me to babysit.

Goes up to the front.

Elaborately pays.

Fights with the driver.

Agrees with the driver.

Comes back.

Gets off a mere four blocks later.

Before he does, he kicks his bag from under the seat, shoulders it, unties all the bungee straps, deposits each one in his deep garage-mechanic-uniform pockets, removes the parrot cage along with himself.

Doors close. On goes the bus.

All that for what? All that for what? A four block ride with a parrot cage?

I was just here sitting across the aisle from the whole show, all alone in this section of the bus me, and the man just left the cage with the birds for me to babysit (I guess, since nothing was said) when he went up to talk to the driver, and then four blocks later etc....

Well. All that all just happened just now.

Or she was a nonspeaking woman, who had an anti-cracking cup.

Gabriel. Delilah. Mikey. Parker Rose. Lady T.

WHO WANTS POPCORN? asks a cluster of teenagers in the back of the bus.

I DO pipes up a man wearing a stuffed horse tied around his chin.

I kid not, I saw this man on the bus, this being later in the day, with a stuffed horse tied to his chin like a marching band helmet would be, chin tied y'know, so that the stuffed horse essentially rode atop the man's head.

When the popcorn is slow in coming, the man adds, in all capital letters: "HEY, WHERE IS MY POPCORN? THE HORSEMAN WANTS HIS POPCORN!"

Big appreciative laugh from the teenagers.

Meanwhile, the four feral children with unibrows all caw their feral sister off at the bus stop, all of them tumbling around the lawn of their yesterday, mistaking it for the sidewalk of today.

At least, though, when they got off, (the cluster of teenagers not the feral children), they gave a very, very, very, very admirably jumbo-sized bag of popcorn away to the Horseman. Wow, I mean, I really didn't know they sold bags of popcorn that large. Largest bag of popcorn I'd ever seen in all my life, in all my time on Earth, largest popcorn bag from any grocery store, any movie theater, any popcorn bag manufacturing plant, anywhere, period. The ultimate end result of capitalism in terms of popcorn sales, this bag of popcorn was. Wow, but it was big.

You should've seen. You should've seen. If you like popcorn at all, in any way shape or form, you should've been there, and you should've seen.

That's the best line in *The Virginian* by Owen Wister, by the way, where the narrator goes all: "You should've seen the palace, and sat there."

Pro tip: jump into the nearest swimming pool to prevent spontaneous combustion.

Just Mom and me cuz Dad left over Mom's increasing weight and the rambling fall of the interior of what you could barely call a house.

Horseman merrily eating more popcorn than he's ever had; he's so happy with the popcorn his teeth have developed a bright new shine for all the dozens of times he smiles as he chews so, so, so gleeful between huge heaping handfuls.

Thank you very much, ladies and gentlemen.

This has been a partial list of all I ever think about on the bus even though these others try to interfere with my thinking, even though it's all I ever think about when I'm at home, too.

-The End-

Burly Mountain

Eight-year-old Clay was at attention in the wood-paneled playroom, about to sing the Anthem for the Burly Battle for the Mountain Castle.

A castle made of tiny fitting bricks stood on the couch that was a mountain.

A battalion of small green soldiers was poised in the field that was a rug, ready to charge and take the Mountain Castle.

Behind the Mountain Castle's ramparts two dozen thumb-sized wooden kittens were convicted to the castle's defense.

Clay had carved the wooden kittens himself, from knots of birch.

That had been when Clay's father took him deer hunting, and Clay hadn't wanted to kill any deer, and so had gotten lost and not been found for close on three days.

Clay had sheltered in a deadfall then, and eaten leaves and moss, and had hidden from certain unspeakable creatures in the night, and had only a pocketknife to protect him, and to wile the time, carving kittens.

But the wooden kittens had been the only good thing to come from the incident, and otherwise Clay didn't like to think of that bad time deer hunting.

Now he was in the playroom. Not safe. But at least indoors.

And just now it was time for the Anthem for the Burly Battle for the Mountain Castle.

Clay raised his left hand in the air, his remaining three fingers thereon shot up in a signal known only to him.

He sang soft and full of proud grief:

"And there were one hundred soldiers
with machine guns and grenades
off to destroy the Mountain Castle of the wooden kittens
and the wooden kittens were so scared to die

their little wooden eyes got really big
and their little wooden hearts beat really fast
cause they didn't have anything
to defend themselves from being killed
in the Burly Battle for the Mountain Castle
except their little wooden claws!"

Clay trailed off. The playroom closet was installed in the far wall, and the unspeakable creature in the closet now reached a curling tentacle full of teeth under the closet door. Then tapped the end of the tentacle against the door's grainy wood.

Tap tap tap

And clacked a few of the sets of teeth.

Clack clack clack.

The as-of-yet-to-this-day-unseen creature in the closet must've been out of its hole in the rear of the closet behind the row of Clay's father's old workboots for a few hours because Clay hadn't heard the creature come from its hole with that rustling it made.

Clay hadn't heard that sound!

Not in the time that'd gone by since he'd come down to the playroom after his Saturday breakfast cereal to see the Battle for the Mountain Castle to its fiery end.

The unspeakable creature in the closet, though, was why Clay felt so unsafe playing in the playroom.

Clay crouched and did a somersault that brought him further from the closet and close to a pile of handy rosewood blocks with the alphabet carved on their fronts. He caught up the handiest block, and threw. It clack-clacked against the closet door and bounced back toward Clay.

The creature in the closet withdrew its tentacle full of teeth.

"Leave! Me! Alone!" shouted Clay. Then he waited. And then there was the rustle that meant the creature had gone back into its hole.

Then there was the kind of quiet that Clay knew much too well, the kind of quiet always left by a brush with an unspeakable creature.

In his pocket, Clay fiddled sweating fingers over a book of matches.

He finally murmured: "I hate playing in the playroom."

For Clay knew the creature in the closet would someday just simply come out and tear him up and chew him up and spit him out. And then he would be in the dark for real, and never able to play again.

But, for the moment, he returned to the anthem:

"Oh brave little wooden kittens
look out you don't get killed
when your castle booms
look out you don't get killed
and taken up to paradise
so you must fight really hard to survive
little wooden kittens
in the burly battle
the burly, burly, burly battle
yes, the Burly Battle for the Mountain Castle!!!"

Clay licked his lips, and his smile crept out half-evil, and he tried to quash its shadowed side by wetting his eyes and looking to the hapless wooden kittens, then by blinking up into and up into and up into and up into the epic landscape of the sheetrock ceiling.

So many formations to walk through and explore in that ceiling, if someone stared hard enough, if the world was upside-down enough, if one grew miniature enough because of, for example, a ray beam that could make someone very, very, very small.

-The End-

Burnt Beach Parking Lot

A foreign-born woman maneuvers her way around a puddle in the parking lot near Gil's blue dead car.

She's moving from the bathroom to the beach.

She could get her husband to give Gil's blue dead car a jump but Gil won't ask.

Let them ask Gil. Later.

Gil'll put up the hood and stand there forlorn, jumper cables tangled in one hand.

But later.

Maybe not even with them.

Because it's still seven hours before nightfall and Gil, he's got nowhere he's gotta be, no goal or map or plan. He once had a goal but he scored it without being fully satisfied and then he just didn't go looking for another goal, and he once had a map but it tore, and he once had a plan but God laughed, and the foreign-born couple, they probably do got somewhere they're going because they apparently shipped their car across the ocean from the looks of the license and that country sticker, and Gil's gotta discern if they even should be bothered, and the rule on that game is if they leave the beach parking lot before Gil discerns them then they're free to go, which is fair enough.

For now, Gil wants the distant cliff face to talk, and they're having a mental battle about it, the cliff face and Gil, that Gil's sure not winning because there's nothing mental going on on the cliff face's side of things but anyway Gil still wants the cliff face to talk because the cliff face is far enough away that its voice would no doubt boom loud enough if it spoke. Gil can see where the eyes, ears, nose, and mouth are. Gil wants the cliff face to tell him what it's like to crumble for centuries, instead of just boring old less-than-a-century. The cliff face could at least say to Gil what the loving hug of the ocean, in its turn, says to the cliff face, roaring moment after roaring moment.

Gil reaches back in the backseat and takes a love letter out of the in box. He reads it. He snatches a red marker from the dashboard and writes along the bottom of the letter in a flippant scrawl: *Do not respond!*

He doesn't actually put an exclamation point but instead a pair of parentheses in which he spells out the words "exclamation" and "point."

He reaches back and puts the love letter in the out box. Only three hundred and thirty-some-odd love letters left to go.

Gil takes the cigarette that's been burning in the ashtray and drags from it. The taste is filthy, like pulling a breath from a stick. Gil's pet garter snake, Little Loo, coiled amongst the jumper cables in the passenger seat, coughs once, a snake's cough. Gil taps the cigarette out the window because Gil's afraid the ashes will somehow set the car on fire if Gil uses the ashtray too much.

Gil's wound up that way.

So.

Yes, indeed.

Gil'll just be here.

Crumbling.

Smoking.

Sorting his love letters.

Trying to get the cliff face to talk.

Discerning who'll have no qualm about helping him.

Here in the parking lot.

By the beach.

And he thanks God he'll only be doing the crumbling part for less-than-a-century.

Unlike certain cliff faces.

At that last four word thought, Gil lets go with a dry chuckle, a chuckle that, come to think of it, would keep on going, and it would keep on going, and it would keep on going on and on and on, going on and on down through the coming (troubled) years.

-The End-

Burnt Surfer

Andy: hard, scary, a burnt surfer.

He had a grim fight with his girlfriend about how best to dispose of a barrel of rotting sausages they'd bought fresh.

His girlfriend said she'd leave him if he didn't throw the barrel of rotting sausages off of a cliff into the sea.

He tried to reason with her but she'd drank far too much coffee in her time and kept adding new tracks to confuse the Argument Train.

Soooooooooooooo there Andy went, one o'clock in the morning, dragging the barrel of rotting sausages along the coastal road.

Headlights splashed him but thankfully no one stopped to ask what the fuck.

Andy tried sometimes to roll the barrel but it spun to the left always. Perhaps the sausages were more moldy and fused together on one end of things than the other. *On the left end of things*, Andy thought to the tune of a grumble that was in turn in tune with an old grunge song's melody Andy had once upon a time known much better.

He finally got to the cliff edge. Now it was 3.30 a.m. but Andy was suddenly substantially frightened that the barrel, once dropped, would hit a night surfer.

The cliff's bottom was a particularly delicate and deadly place to surf and Andy had never before in his life met any hardcore night surfers there in Penniforth Cove.

Buuuuuuuuuuuuuuut, then again, his best friend Nigel did sometimes get ahold of crystal meth, and would go surf past midnight in places where he (Nigel) shouldn't have.

Just go ahead, just go ahead, just go ahead, thought Andy, his brain making a snapping sound, and he kicked the barrel of rotting sausages over the cliff.

Sausages, sausages, sausages, thought Andy in his dreams that night.

"Nooooooooooooo!" he wailed, launching from sleep in a slow-motion slipstream of sweat bubbles and ice claws.

The next day, in the crush of afternoon sunlight, Andy was trying to get his girlfriend to walk a mile for once when he saw his best friend, Nigel, waltzing out of the movie theater surrounded by his illegitimate children.

"Nigel!" Andy called, and Nigel looked up and smiled a smile that spoke of much time spent ricocheting before it had arrived.

"You're alive!" Andy yelled, his yell full of his relieved grin, and his high sliding back to hiiiiiiiilarity.

-The End-

Bus Minx

A fire had sprung up far across the dog park.
And he knew his cigarettes had done the trick.
He had a dream fight on the bus.
But his fists were dream fists and didn't fly fast enough.
Dregs.
Bits of slate on the shuffle between one crevice then another.
The people who ride buses.
I shouldn't talk.
I'm one of them.
I am, in fact, the original Bus Minx.
"No, Hardinger. The way you see yourself is not the way you actually are."

-The End-

Business Leaders of Michigan

The Business Leaders of Michigan all awoke surprised to find themselves sleeping in the same motel room together. Some of the Business Leaders of Michigan were even in the same beds as others of the Business Leaders of Michigan and there was even some awkward nudity. Thus it was that the Business Leaders of Michigan did no business, nor even spoke words from mouths, for the first hour of the Monday morning.

The Business Leaders of Michigan got dressed in smart business clothes and had a shower apiece and gathered on the sidewalk out in front of the motel for a head count.

They ran through a little bit of voting then, on the way to breakfast.

They voted not to buy any tools unless they'd be paid for by the job budget. They voted to wait to let one of the members of the Business Leaders of Michigan have a quick vomit in the bushes while still remaining anonymous. They voted to say "have a nice day" to passing members of the general public with the full sunrise intention of saying it like saying "have a nice day" instead of saying it like saying "fuck you."

They decided on two benches for the plaza that centered the ⱨⱨⱨ ⱨⱨ ⱨⱨⱨⱨ ⱨⱨⱨⱨⱨⱨⱨⱨⱨⱨⱨⱨ ⱨⱨⱨⱨ ⱨⱨⱨⱨ ⱨⱨⱨⱨ ⱨⱨⱨⱨ ⱨⱨⱨⱨⱨⱨⱨⱨⱨⱨ ⱨⱨⱨ ⱨⱨⱨ Business Leaders of Michigan.

They decided that they'd get brass inlays for the elevators, and with a bit of Business Leaders of Michigan wit, they decided it would be Scandanavians installing the brass inlays. *Ha, Ha, Ha!* laughed the Business Leaders of Michigan in the backs of their minds. *Scandinavians! Ha! Ha!*

At lunch, !!OH, LUNCH!!, the Business Leaders of Michigan decided amongst themselves they had once heard tell of luncheons of business times of old in which were had three martinis or anyway a martini upon sitting down, a martini with soup and salad, and a martini with the entree. But those times are long gone and the Business Leaders of Michigan are even going forward with the idea of speculating a future where they skip the coffee mugs, even, as they peer into the coffee mugs thinking how unimaginable having no coffee mug would be but how that must be a frontier in some dimension of business or t'other, tho maybe not Michigan's dimension. But then again, they really did have to stop intaking so much caffeine so as not to cinder their adrenals.

Meanwhile, as some of the Business Leaders of Michigan looked into the depths of their coffee mugs contemplating a divorce from the coffee therein, others of the Business Leaders of Michigan who were already long past coffee watched salad come across their salad plates and be devoured, salad like a song that went *green lettuce, red lettuce, green lettuce, radish, sliced avocado, half-a-toasted-bagel, steak-cooked cauliflower*.

The Business Leaders of Michigan refused two offers from other tables in the place of luncheoning, one offer being a bottle of vinegar and one offer being a merger between Stimso Container Limited and Mandt Materials Incorporated, but before the waiter had finished saying "The gentlemen at that table would like to buy your table a bottle of milk to go with your coffees and let you know that the index 110% indicates Mandt Materials Incorp—" the Business Leaders of Michigan all burst out laughing because that would never happen and wasn't even theoretically do-able business-wise, nor contractually speaking, and plus 110% was just plain straight up bad math.

On their way out the swinging doors and away from the smells of cooking, the Business Leaders of Michigan slunk guilty and not-so-agile past the cloakroom because most of them had neglected to wear a suitcoat and the rest of them had lost their coat check stubs in the general hurricane of napkins whipped from laps and wiped across lips.

The Business Leaders of Michigan came across an old fat bum. The bum had hung a plastic bucket around his neck, marked "God Bless" on the front of the bucket, and then had gone to sleep sitting up in a doorway in a puddle of his own making, halfway waking only occasionally to sneeze, each sneeze causing a sharp clatter of coin from the bucket's interior.

The Business Leaders of Michigan voted quickly to ignore the bum and then quickly reversed that vote against the wailing of their consciences and voted to find the bum a tiny house, guesstimating that'd run 10k tops. After all, they were the Business Leaders of Michigan leading the business of Michigan and the old fat bum just did nothing but sleep in a puddle of his own piss all the day through, so the least they could do is find him a house, albeit small, albeit resource intensive.

At afternoon snack time, the Business Leaders of Michigan, every last one of them, thought it would be best to order the Vegetable Platter, that being most of the world's known vegetables grilled and collected on a lotus-shaped bed of iceberg lettuce.

But instead, all the Business Leaders of Michigan, every last one of them, could not resist ordering *Vertical*, it's alternate title being *Sixteen Ounce Cinnamon Roll Atop A Six-Stack of Two-Inch-Thick Chocolate Chip Pancakes*.

The Business Leaders of Michigan thought of Money, thought of her fondly in remembrance, called her a Sweetheart Deal under their breaths but not under their breaths in any sort of snide way.

The Business Leaders of Michigan thought of Rodney, and thinking of Rodney was always mission critical.

The Business Leaders of Michigan ran for the farmers' market on the corner where they were sure to be somewhat unruly and buy more foodstuffs to eat, especially for lunch, ah yes, lunch.

There among the Business Leaders of Michigan was a growing sense of pride, though. They decided Business in general needed to sharpen up its ethics. What was the point of being a "good" businessman if you fucked people over to get your way? The Business Leaders of Michigan proposed an oath that would be like the Hippocratic Oath. Except it would be called the "Michiganocratic Oath."

The Michiganocratic Oath would basically state: "Do no harm when you do your Business, dipshit." Tho it was uncouth and not aboveboard, they still felt they needed the "dipshit" part to jar themselves and others from any apathy that might glaze them over after a long day, say a 10-hour day, at the office.

The Business Leaders of Michigan stood beneath the telephone pole and wondered whether within the telephone pole were lots of moving parts and wondered whether the telephone pole had any low hanging fruit and wondered whether they could from then on run things up the telephone pole instead of running things up the flagpole and then they argued the telephone pole's trajectory and thought about whether they missed talking on phones back when they had a meatier receiver to hold in their hands as a stopgap between those more onion-ring-ish receivers (LUNCH!!) and the thin slices of meatless toast (BRUNCH!!) they carried now, phone-wise.

The Business Leaders of Michigan drank a smoothie, one smoothie amongst all of them, one sip apiece and then the smoothie shared onward, and they soon decided "bananas not oranges" and "Vitamin C but not raspberry."

Soon after that smoothie, the Business Leaders of Michigan decided to try their business at water recovery and devised a desalination pipeline that would come in from the ocean until all the water therein was freshwater by the time it reached the inland place it wanted to go.

THE BLOM, in all caps, they thought they might call themselves for short, and it was put to a vote.

Just as soon as the vote circulated, though, THE BLOM decided that THE BLOM was undignified per an acronym and reverted to calling themselves the Business Leaders of Michigan once more, even though sometimes some of the ex-smokers and the secret smokers amongst the Business Leaders of Michigan found their breath running out right about at the "Mi."

The Business Leaders of Michigan decided to do an initiative tiger-team-wise to solar panel every business in Michigan.

The Business Leaders of Michigan encouraged bike riding and rode their bikes from then on, from the moment they started encouraging bike riding onward.

They were the Business Leaders of Michigan. They had eyes. They had ears. They knew the planet had gotten too hot. The planet they were standing on.

"Why can't every coastal town sponsor a rain-and-food-forest via a desalination pipeline?" asked the Business Leaders of Michigan.

Back from the wars, the Business Leaders of Michigan found themselves in a pub.

Back from the wars, the Business Leaders of Michigan found themselves in a pool.

Back from the wars, the Business Leaders of Michigan found themselves satisfied with how businesses in Michigan were going generally. Hardware stores were on the upswing, which meant building, which meant families, which meant retail sales.

Tⅼⅰⱴ Ɒⱶ𝖑ⅰⅰⱴⱶⱶ Ⅼⱶⱶⅼⱶⅰⅰ ⱶⅼ ⅳⅰⅰ'ⅰⅰⅰ𝖌ⅰⅰ ⅰⅰⅰⱱ ⅰⅰ ⅰⅰ 𝖈ⱶⅰⅰⅰⱨ𝖑ⅰ ⱶⅰⱨⱶⅰⱶ ⅰⅰⅰ ⅰ bench somehow since the bench was not itself circular. A plaque on the bench spelled out a memoriam of a former bunch of the Business Leaders of Michigan from the 1940s who were now all retired with golden parachutes.

At 3 a.m. the Business Leaders of Michigan put an outer space continuum of stars and novas on their wall-length television and decide to angle for 4 a.m. when for sure no other business leaders would be awake. But then again, sleep in a bed sounds so delicious that the Business Leaders of Michigan have to take a vote whether to sleep without sleeping because tomorrow their course starts on how to be better business leaders with more hyperlocal ideation to put themselves in the loop at least knee deep.

IMPORTANT: CAPITALISM MUST BE COMPASSIONATE, the Business Leaders of Michigan posted on a piece of typing paper outside each of their individual corner offices after lunch (!!) and the cut and pasting of the signage takes at least twenty minutes so that means lunch, oh yeah baby, was, like, all told, an hour and twenty minutes for that day.

CAPITALISM MUST FIRST DO NO HARM becomes the Business Leaders of Michigan's Michiganocratic Oath in official documents from then on as well.

Down dip their tailbones into the rolls and ridges of their office chairs and they jab around inside their mouths with their tongue tips for remaining bits of lunch.

These then, the Business Leaders of Michigan, stop to take an official count of themselves but they each lose track when trying to count themselves, each of them themselves that is, and the whole official count idea proves low on scaleability.

The Business Leaders of Michigan wonder if it rains outside often with the cars sounding the way they do going by the headquarters, the cars' tires mingling asphalt with water with air with rolling to create that hopeless, despairing sound.

Documenting the history of themselves and glass on the floor, the Business Leaders of Michigan do so around the historical society table meant to be only a food chain place for discoursing on the history of the headquarters.

The Business Leaders of Michigan went vegan for their health and the environment and their love of animals.

The Business Leaders of Michigan found a stick in the road.

The Business Leaders of Michigan found old minutes of old meetings written in old notebooks with rusted spiral rings and had to take a meeting to reminisce about how wacky their meetings used to be when they had all just gotten their start in business.

The Business Leaders of Michigan suddenly decided they couldn't wait to feel the dip of sleep and thought maybe tomorrow they might sleep the day away. It was cold that winter, for sure, and cold is for being wrapped in blankets.

The Business Leaders of Michigan got back on track with not minding beer bottles smashed across the floor of their caravan in a pan out of hand against sullen man.

The Business Leaders of Michigan came upon an encampment, a place that never should have been. There were broken shopping carts that had run out of wheels, shopping cart after shopping cart. There were needles scattered like cheatgrass. There were tents that had been half-sewn. There were tents that it looked like you couldn't go in or out of. There was a diamond glimpsed that quickly turned into just another shard of broken glass after a second glance from the Business Leaders of Michigan.

-The End-

But If The

But if the time should come
that you gain ground
going downhill
toward white sands
best watch the rabbits
leaping across the green lanes
they have blurred eyes
for falling every spring.

-The End-

But Justice

Frank sought justice on the train. A burly drunk with an overlarge baseball cap took up two seats even though there were people standing. Another man had an oxygen tank and a tube mustaching his nose. Frank himself was standing, and even on his bad foot. There was no justice on the train.

Frank sought ideals in the rain. But the drops hit too soft or too hard. The frequency never seemed to flow. Sometimes, Frank was forced to wear a raincoat. Or when he wore a raincoat there wasn't enough rain to warrant it. There were no ideals in the rain.

Frank sought manners at the table on the train. But no one remembered about elbows. Frank's Aunt Larry talked with his or her mouth full. Frank himself could never remember which fork. There were no manners at the table on the train.

After that, Frank sought nothing whatsoever. He stayed indoors just sitting around the apartment and just listening to the ticking of the clock and just watching the wallpaper peel with burning sepia eyes, wielding a never-ending series of brown cigarettes he had the people deliver with his groceries, the cigarettes always jutting from between fingers #2 and #3.

-The End-

But Love

Frank sought Love in the season of its birth. But there were too many baubles and lights and piles of junk wrapped in giddy paper. Empathy and Sympathy and Fondness kept opening different avenues. All feelings including Love were invisible. Love's Practitioners thought they were so rad. But there was no Love in the season of its birth.

Frank sought Helping Hands in a shop. But no one who clerked the shop spoke English. The patrons of the shop had open wallets and open purses and slack looks. The shop was stocked with nothing Frank wanted. Frank could barely breathe for boredom. There were no Helping Hands in the shop.

Frank sought Starlight in the stables. But the horses of the stables whinnied and shied, nervous about Frank's presence. Clouds weighted with snow were blotting the sky overhead. There was straw and manure and the occasional fainting goat. A stable boy asked Frank what the fuck Frank was doing there. There was no Starlight in the stables.

After that, Frank sought nothing whatsoever. He just drank thin blue gins and wandered the city shivering, slipping on icy spots, hurting his tailbone, getting more blind from the cold, until he came upon folks singing, in semi-unison, a song he'd never heard before, and even though Frank wasn't accustomed to it, the song sounded okay.

-The End-

But Peace

Frank sought peace in the countryside. But the farmer killed the hen, the planes bombed the farm and killed the farmer, the men with dead eyes hiding in the hills surrounding the farm hit the planes with rockets and the planes fell down and obliterated the sheep in the farm's fields. There was no peace in the countryside.

Frank sought logic in the town. But the mayor was dead, the councilmen were dirty, the populace was diseased. The town fountain was full of blood, which made a sludge with the ever-falling ash. The town square was round. There was no logic in the town.

Frank sought compassion in a cave in a cliff. But the bats of the cave regarded him with indifference, and spooked him. At the cave's very back were more men hiding behind dead eyes. They had twitchy women, who had dead eyes too. Frank himself had brought along a handgun and a hatchet. There was no compassion in the cave in the cliff.

After that, Frank sought he didn't know what. He sat on a cold stump in the forest and picked purple fungi and ate it hoping to get sick and die but instead he was just sitting around seeing things in too many colors and wondering what he didn't know and doing he didn't know what and not knowing quite what to do besides smile and laugh and sit and think thoughts that wended around and around without conclusion.

-The End-

Butcher Manners

Butcher cuts himself on the cutting wheel while slicing Harry's ham slices. The butcher bleeds all over Harry's ham slices while Harry watches. But then the butcher bags the ham up and gives the ham to Harry anyway.

Harry slinks away and the butcher slinks away.

Both too embarrassed to say anything much beyond "three dollars," "here you go" and a pair of thanks.

Harry carries home his bagful of ham and blood. Embarrassed all the way, not sure about all that blood. But the bag seems to be holding.

The butcher goes home to his family, too. Also embarrassed. Sullen through dinner.

The butcher demands his wife dish him up only the broccoli, and not any meatloaf.

-The End-

Butty the Gunny, Bunny the Gutty, or Anyway, Gutty the Bunny

Each Wednesday that grew tragic in Gutty the Bunny's able mind, the Wednesdays he'd feel little spiny shadows fuzz around his long ears and snicker through his fear to collect at his cottontail, Gutty would snake a furtive expedition to Farmer Will's western meadow, looking for the Muddy Cat.

The Muddy Cat was a brown color, and never made any effort past that first mild effort that wasn't even really an effort to kill Gutty. And so now these days, Gutty the Bunny and the Muddy Cat would engage in desultory discussion over the Rock-Throwing Hermit and just what to do about him. Both had been pinged more than ten times by the Hermit, who lived in the nearby ash-strewn woods, in one of the caves.

"We could follow the Hermit," said Gutty, wondering why he only had these conversations on Wednesdays.

"True," said the Muddy Cat. "We follow him to his cave, wherever he's got it, and then steal his food so he starves."

Gutty the Bunny and the Muddy Cat would kick ideas around like that, then go back to their respective homes.

Gutty the Bunny knew what showers under waterfalls were about, but he never used the waterfall showers, bathing only in the river maybe once a week.

Like luck flicked up under my dry tongue, Gutty the Bunny would think.

Once there were two sons of a miner. They watched how their miner father was treated by his mining job and determined not to follow in his footsteps. They hung red bandannas bulging with glossy fruit on the ends of walking sticks, and set off with the sticks set on their shoulder tops. They fancied themselves in search of fortune. Their names were Donner and Dibble.

Donner wound up in the travel business in Nevada and was just always throwing a lot of parties.

Dibble, however, became an interesting gent indeed. He took to performing on the street. Busking was the technical term for street performing, at least in Dibble's days. He invented a combination organ, harp, and tuba, and called it an "orhatu."

Dibble's problem, though, was that he gradually preferred busking on cleaner and cleaner streets and so worked his way into the countryside where there weren't many passersby to toss him money.

Which is how, one day, Gutty the Bunny happened to hear the strains of the orhatu's single song, and it was then and there Gutty the Bunny came up with lyrics to go along with the strains.

Christmas-light-lit Christmas tree
this morning in a far window
got our bath in the river
went laughing through the hollow
sometimes we sit there
having trouble not screaming
sometimes we sit there and smile
sometimes we chew over a hard-fought-for carrot
but we'll only do that a little while.

Wednesday of the next week was another utter failure of a day. If Gutty the Bunny works too hard rooting up lettuce he misses out on sitting watching clouds. But then if Gutty the Bunny breathes in every moment with the clouds he still forgets their different shapes. Usually, it only takes a day before the feeling of this or that marvelous nuance has vanished. Gutty the Bunny thinks of asking one of his brothers for some of their lettuce. He's never sure what to do. He doesn't quite belong in any warren, including one he once made for himself. Gutty the Bunny is partial to things he doesn't own, and hateful of things he does. Gutty the Bunny does his philosophic business with no triumph in sight. Gutty the Bunny doesn't enjoy outside forces shaping him but he lets himself be shaped even so. What choice does he have? He is Gutty. He scratches some of his thoughts on a patch of bare earth in the forest but when he fills the patch with crazy, crooked bunny words he'll just have to go to the trouble of finding another patch.

Then it was the Wednesday after that. Gutty the Bunny sat with the Muddy Cat. The Muddy Cat licked at a thorn stuck fast among his right front paw's claws. Both the Muddy Cat and Gutty the Bunny had tried to tug the thorn free, but it was too far stuck down and neither of their teeth sets quite clamped right for the task. So Gutty the Bunny did most of the talking that day, while the Muddy Cat half-listened and licked at the thorn and watched green pus ooze out of the wound surrounding the thorn.

"It doesn't look like the healthiest of wounds," said Gutty the Bunny at last. "Why not get Your Master to pull the thorn out?"

"I would," said the Muddy Cat, "but My Master has up and moved in with the Hermit, and when I tried to approach My Master, the Hermit threw rocks to keep me away."

"Oh," said Gutty the Bunny. He looked across the green fields at the blue clouds and clicked over and over the thought of how much he didn't like Wednesdays.

"What is a Wednesday?" the Muddy Cat asked, when Gutty spoke his thoughts aloud.

"It's a square on a calendar," said Gutty the Bunny.

"What's a calendar?" asked the Muddy Cat.

Gutty the Bunny shrugged. "You're the one that's been indoors in your span of time. You would probably know, much better than me."

But the Muddy Cat also shrugged, and said nothing, and grew distracted, and then went back to licking his wound.

-The End-

Buzzing Hermit

Walking back from watching the sunset at his uncle's memorial bench, that old battered bench by the cliff edge with the ocean a deep fishy mystery far below, Croppy Floyd encountered the mean, bad, blue, buzzing hermit that lived at the back of the cemetery along the never-used public footpath in a tin shack, literally a shack made of tins as the British know the word to mean.

The hermit was leaning against the corner of the shack, chewing on what could have been a bit of rag or a bit of bone, and the hermit was poised.

Poised as though waiting for Croppy.

"Been to see the sea?" asked the hermit in a quiet voice of lazy hate.

Croppy stuttered in his step, and had a quick stare at the hermit, and said a hasty apology, and hitched off along the path.

"Don't ever come back," the hermit advised after Croppy, which Croppy could only assume the hermit knew full well was fraught advice, since Croppy visited his uncle's memorial bench weekly, and sometimes daily.

-The End-

By the Light of the British Atlas of Places

I got nice and tiredly drunk on the old wine, at a wooden table versus a fat candle, and read out town descriptions to Minette, read them out with stirring yet dulcet tones, from the British Atlas of Places.

-The End-

Author Bio

Guy J. Jackson is a would-be moviemaker currently dwelling in Los Angeles, though his essence can also be found on YouTube, TikTok, and Instagram. He wrote and starred in a feature film regarding the former of those places and thus aptly entitled *Los Angeles Overnight*. His first book of short stories was *Drink the Rest of That,* and it can still be found in several of the places where short stories are sold.

ROUNDFIRE
BOOKS

FICTION

Historical fiction that lives

Put simply, we publish great stories. Whether it's literary or popular, a gentle tale or a pulsating thriller, the connecting theme in all Roundfire fiction titles is that once you pick them up you won't want to put them down.
If you have enjoyed this book, why not tell other readers by posting a review on your preferred book site.

Recent bestsellers from Roundfire are:

The Bookseller's Sonnets
Andi Rosenthal
The Bookseller's Sonnets intertwines three love stories with a
tale of religious identity and mystery spanning five hundred
years and three countries.
Paperback: 978-1-84694-342-3 ebook: 978-184694-626-4

Birds of the Nile
An Egyptian Adventure
N.E. David
Ex-diplomat Michael Blake wanted a quiet birding trip up the
Nile – he wasn't expecting a revolution.
Paperback: 978-1-78279-158-4 ebook: 978-1-78279-157-7

Blood Profit$
The Lithium Conspiracy
J. Victor Tomaszek, James N. Patrick, Sr.
The blood of the many for the profits of the few… *Blood Profit$*
will take you into the cigar-smoke-filled room where American
policy and laws are really made.
Paperback: 978-1-78279-483-7 ebook: 978-1-78279-277-2

The Burden
A Family Saga
N.E. David
Frank will do anything to keep his mother and father
apart. But he's carrying baggage – and it might just weigh
him down …
Paperback: 978-1-78279-936-8 ebook: 978-1-78279-937-5

The Cause
Roderick Vincent
The second American Revolution will be a fire lit from
an internal spark.
Paperback: 978-1-78279-763-0 ebook: 978-1-78279-762-3

Don't Drink and Fly
The Story of Bernice O'Hanlon: Part One
Cathie Devitt
Bernice is a witch living in Glasgow. She loses her way in her
life and wanders off the beaten track looking for the garden of
enlightenment.
Paperback: 978-1-78279-016-7 ebook: 978-1-78279-015-0

Gag
Melissa Unger
One rainy afternoon in a Brooklyn diner, Peter Howland
punctures an egg with his fork. Repulsed, Peter pushes the
plate away and never eats again.
Paperback: 978-1-78279-564-3 ebook: 978-1-78279-563-6

The Master Yeshua
The Undiscovered Gospel of Joseph
Joyce Luck
Jesus is not who you think he is. The year is 75 CE. Joseph
ben Jude is frail and ailing, but he has a prophecy to fulfil ...
Paperback: 978-1-78279-974-0 ebook: 978-1-78279-975-7

On the Far Side, There's a Boy
Paula Coston

Martine Haslett, a thirty-something 1980s woman, plays hard on the fringes of the London drag club scene until one night which prompts her to sign up to a charity. She writes to a young Sri Lankan boy, with consequences far and long.
Paperback: 978-1-78279-574-2 ebook: 978-1-78279-573-5

Tuareg
Alberto Vazquez-Figueroa

With over 5 million copies sold worldwide, *Tuareg* is a classic adventure story from best-selling author Alberto Vazquez-Figueroa, about honour, revenge and a clash of cultures.
Paperback: 978-1-84694-192-4

Readers of ebooks can buy or view any of these bestsellers by clicking on the live link in the title. Most titles are published in paperback and as an ebook. Paperbacks are available in traditional bookshops. Both print and ebook formats are available online.

Find more titles and sign up to our readers' newsletter at www.collectiveinkbooks.com/fiction